WICKED
GAMES

WICKED GAMES

My Year of Submission

KELLY LAWRENCE

BLACK
LACE

2 4 6 8 10 9 7 5 3 1

First published in 2013 by Black Lace, an imprint of Ebury Publishing
A Random House Group Company

Addresses for companies within the Random House Group can
be found at: www.randomhouse.co.uk

The Random House Group Limited Reg. No. 954009

A CIP catalogue record for this book is available from the British Library

The Random House Group Limited supports the Forest Stewardship
Council® (FSC®), the leading international forest-certification organisation. Our
books carrying the FSC label are printed on FSC®-certified paper. FSC is the only
forest-certification scheme supported by the leading environmental organisations,
including Greenpeace. Our paper procurement policy can be found
at www.randomhouse.co.uk/environment

MIX
Paper from
responsible sources
FSC® C016897

Printed and bound by Clays Ltd, St Ives PLC

ISBN 9780753541715

To buy books by your favourite authors and register for offers visit:
www.randomhouse.co.uk

For Valerie – the first one was always going to be yours.

Preface

I laid my cheek on the leather, my hands overhead, pulling at the restraints he had bound me with. I fought to steady myself, even as my breath came in nervous pants. My heart pounded. I was terrified of what was to come – yet, at the same time, desperately excited.

The back of my neck tingled where he had bitten it, making me crave his touch again. I pulled back against my bonds, wanting to lean into him, but he had stepped away, leaving me bereft and yearning for him.

'Lift her skirt,' I heard him command, his voice thick with desire.

I felt gentle hands tugging up my dress and revealing my ass in its skimpy thong. I hadn't been expecting anybody but him to see it, and felt completely exposed. My face burned with embarrassment, yet at the same time I was trembling in anticipation of whatever wicked game he now had planned.

Even as I gave my body up to him, my mind was reeling, wondering: how the hell did I end up here?

Chapter One

I looked at my line manager in complete and total disbelief. She rambled on about the New Year initiative, oblivious to my confusion.

'Hang on' – I raised a hand to stop her mid-flow (trust me, if I hadn't, she would have gone on for ever) – 'Margaret wants me on the cover of the prospectus? I'm the "new face of Adult Education"?'

Amanda, my plump, friendly line manager, nodded like an eager puppy.

'You do remember that last year she said I was "not presenting a professional enough image"?'

Amanda grimaced.

'Yes, well. She did spot you dressed in hot pants, having a Champagne breakfast on your way to a hen weekend. After you had been off sick all week.'

I had to concede she had a point. And without wanting to blow my own trumpet (though someone had to), I understood why she had chosen me. I was the only female tutor under thirty who didn't dress like an old spinster, and I scrubbed up OK. Although I personally thought the usual prospectus pictures of smiling, happy students worked adequately. If the powers that be were putting a young, pretty tutor on the cover to attract students, they were going to feel short-changed when they ended up in a class with seventy-year-old Mike, who had movable dentures and a penchant for pickled onions and pepperoni sandwiches.

Where on earth was I supposed to find the time for impromptu photo shoots? I grumbled away to myself as Amanda rattled on yet again about our targets for the coming year and the importance of getting attendance figures in on time. Although I loved my job as a full-time adult literacy tutor, it ate severely into my personal life; for every hour I spent teaching, I seemed to spend three writing about it, recording it, updating learner profiles and marking work. I certainly didn't want to give up a Saturday morning to have my photo taken.

'. . . the new HR manager will be there. He's a total hottie.'

My ears perked up at that – more at the unexpectedness of Amanda using the phrase 'total hottie' than anything else. I was in no mood for men, having not long finished an ill-fated relationship with a toy boy gym instructor who had looked like Adonis but turned out to have a serious steroid addiction. But a little window shopping might make my Saturday morning more interesting.

I finally agreed, although I knew that once Margaret – our pit bull-like student resources manager – had decided something, there was very little choice in the matter.

Once home that evening, I gratefully sank into my fluffy

zebra-print cushions, glass of rosé wine in one hand, stack of lesson plans in the other, and kicked off my pumps.

At twenty-six, I had been living alone in my apartment for three years. I was happy enough; I was proud of my job, loved my flat, and had some great friends and an active social life. I was rarely short of a date, but I had never found 'the one'. Not that I was necessarily on the lookout for him. If I was honest, what I really missed about being in a relationship was the lashings of regular sex.

Not – however – that I regarded myself as any kind of sexual connoisseur. My first sexual relationship, which had begun at the age of sixteen, had culminated in an ill-advised marriage at eighteen, which had consisted of a dress from Topshop, a trip to the local registry office and a honeymoon with our friends in Blackpool. Hardly the stuff of dreams. It perhaps wasn't surprising that the flush of puppy love had fast faded and ended in an amicable divorce at twenty-one. Both of us initially virgins, the most adventurous our sex life had ever got was probably doggie-style with the lights on. I had been happy enough at the time, but as the relationship ended and I realised my friends were all light years away from me in terms of experience, I began to wonder if I hadn't been missing out, and became eager to broaden my sexual knowledge.

But that was easier said than done. A few flings followed, none of which particularly inspired me sexually. My most recent relationship had been with twenty-year-old Nathan, the steroid-addicted gym instructor, and in spite of my being six years ahead of him in age, he had been miles ahead of me in experience. It was the closest I felt I had ever come to a sexual awakening – whatever that meant in my narrow experience.

Thinking about Nathan made me smile as I lay back on the couch, sipping my wine and staring at my paperwork absent-mindedly as my thoughts drifted back to our short-lived liaison. Although his obsession with bodybuilding and his own appearance had left me cold (the final straw coming when he seriously asked me if his ass looked big in his new jeans), in the bedroom I had had no complaints. I recalled one of the last times we'd had sex, in his apartment after a night out with friends, when he had fucked me into the early hours of the morning. Remembering his hands on my body and his whispered endearments in my ear, his breath hot on my neck as his thrusts had brought me closer to a shuddering climax, I felt my nipples stiffen under the thin cotton of my blouse. I ran my hand over my breasts through the thin material, allowing my arousal to build. The memory of his buff and tanned body rearing over me as he stroked me with expert hands grew sharper, and I closed my eyes. I inched my skirt up to run my hand over my thighs . . .

And groaned as the sudden trill of the phone ringing resounded through my flat, sounding improbably loud. I debated letting the answering machine pick it up, but the moment had passed. Pulling my skirt back down, I leaned over and picked it up.

'How was work? First week back after the Christmas holidays is always tough.' I heard my stepfather's gruff voice and immediately blushed at the interruption. The moment was well and truly ruined now.

'Fine, Dad, how was your day?'

My stepfather worked at the local engineering factory and claimed to hate it, in spite of having been there twenty years and never having had a day off sick. As he launched into a diatribe against his new 'young whippersnapper' manager, I grinned to myself and rolled my eyes, settling back into the cushions and picking up the glass of wine again with my free hand. It might be a long call.

'Hmm . . .' I murmured non-committally as he paused in his ranting, obviously expecting some kind of answer.

My mumbling must have satisfied him, as he carried on immediately where he had left off and I smiled with affection. I adored my stepdad; a typical brawling, working-class Irishman, he had always treated me as his own, making up for a somewhat distant mother who often regarded me with an air of confused disappointment, as if she couldn't quite remember what I was doing there, and wasn't very impressed. As I grew up I often wondered if her lack of maternal affection was because I had been swapped at birth, and consoled myself by imagining I was really a princess, or, as I got older, a celebrity love child. Unfortunately the physical resemblance was evident. I was blessed with my mother's big blue eyes and petite figure, and cursed with her uncontrollable dark curls, which I attempted to wrestle into a chic updo every morning. What the hell I was going to do with it for the prospectus photos in the morning I didn't know.

I sighed as I remembered I had arranged to visit my mother the next day. I would have to go after Margaret had finished with me.

'How's Mum?' I cut into his grumbling. 'I said I'd pop round tomorrow. I might be a bit late, though.' I started to tell him about the photo shoot I had been lassoed into, expecting him to laugh. Instead, he seemed proud.

'I'm sure you'll look very beautiful,' he said, before adding, 'as long as you cover up those bloody tattoos. Why you youngsters today want to deface yourselves I don't know.'

'Not this again, Dad,' I said with a sigh.

I was proud of my small collection of body art: a riot of vines, flowers and butterflies over one shoulder and down the opposite hip and thigh. I thought they were artistic, but my dad considered them an adult extension of my so-called teenage-rebellion stage, which had mostly consisted of sharing bottles of cheap cider with my friends and aimlessly wandering around looking for something mildly illegal to do – hardly a wild child. While I had to concede the tattoos were a little at odds with the demure-teacher image I usually cultivated, I wasn't about to get into a debate with my dad about it.

'I ought to go,' I said now, cutting off his protestations. 'I'm off to see Kimberly this evening and I still have to get changed.'

'Well, have fun, love,' he replied. 'And behave – I know what you two are like when you get together!'

Later that night I sat round my best mate Kimberly's, being very much the opposite of demure, drinking large amounts of wine and giggling at an Adam Sandler movie. She had tried to show me how to French plait my hair in answer to tomorrow's crisis, but we'd given up after she had nearly skewered me with a hairgrip.

As often happened on our girlie nights, the conversation

turned to sex. Kim had been my best friend since the age of ten, although we had precious little in common. I was a teacher, she was a nail technician; where I was horribly disorganised, she bordered on OCD, and whereas I tended to go for 'bad boys' or at least men with some kind of edge to them, Kim went for safe, predictable mummy's boys that she could wrap around her carefully manicured little finger. That meant that she also inevitably became bored. Gary, her current boyfriend, had been around nearly a year and, true to form, she was already getting fed up.

'I thought things were great?' I asked now.

'I don't know,' she sighed. 'Gary's just not doing it for me at the minute. It's the same old routine, every single time; I reckon he even counts his thrusts.'

I giggled. 'At least you're getting some.'

'I thought you had a thing going with Shane?'

Ah, Shane. A mutual friend, also going back to primary school, Shane was the very hot local tattooist who had recently become a 'friend with benefits'. A night out to celebrate my single status after splitting with Nathan had culminated in too many tequila slammers and a fumble on my couch. The next morning, after deciding that we would forget all about our drunken mistake, we had ended up having fast and furious sex in my shower, the warm water cascading over our bodies only adding to the thrill. Yet after the initial passion, our last few encounters had left me wanting, with a nagging sense of needing something more.

I shrugged at Kim. 'I don't think it's right,' I confessed. 'We've been friends so long; I think he's just too familiar. It's not like I get butterflies when I see him.'

'You need to take it back to being "friends with *no* benefits", then.'

'Exactly.'

'Maybe we should try speed dating. They're having a night down the local next week. Get you a new man,' Kim suggested, laughing at the incredulous look on my face.

'No, thanks.'

I couldn't think of anything worse than having to repeat the same three-minute conversation with a queue of strange men. Truth be told, in spite of my growing sexual frustration, I was fairly self-sufficient and didn't feel the need to be in a relationship. Kim's serial boyfriend-hopping baffled me. She was constantly falling in love, only to fall out of it just as quickly, whereas I hadn't felt that for a guy since my starry-eyed first love.

'Mr Right will turn up someday soon and sweep us off our feet, I'm sure,' Kim mock-sighed, making a dramatic sweeping gesture with her hands. 'He's just taking his time.'

'It's the credit crunch,' I quipped. 'He had to sell his charging white horse.'

And we went back to giggling into our wine. I fell into bed a few hours later, happy and relaxed – until I remembered I had to get up in the morning for the photo shoot with Margaret. There went my Saturday lie-in.

My last thought as I drifted off to sleep was Amanda's comment about the new HR manager; I wondered idly if I would agree with her.

Chapter Two

Saturday dawned, grey and unwelcoming, and I reluctantly dragged myself out of bed. I had a minor panic deciding what to wear, discarding the pencil skirt and cardigan I had picked out the previous evening. I finally settled on a grey woollen dress, tonged my dark hair in an attempt to make my curls less unruly, and applied a little more make-up than usual. I was pretty sure that Adult Ed weren't going to stretch to a stylist. I surveyed myself in the mirror and wondered if I looked a touch too sexy; though the dress was on the knee and showed no cleavage, it fit beautifully and clung to every curve. I was confident the new manager would appreciate it, even if Margaret didn't.

The pictures were being taken outside the town hall and I walked the fifteen minutes to the city centre, instantly regretting it when the cold January wind picked up. My hair was going to be ruined. Perhaps I should have attempted Kim's French plait after all.

The photographer and Margaret were waiting outside. It's an ornate entrance, the city's coat of arms painted ostentatiously across the large double doors, and Margaret stood in front of them like a reigning monarch, arms folded.

'Better late than never,' she said drily. I glanced at the clock across the road; it was two minutes past the hour.

Before I could protest a rich, deep voice came up the stairs behind me.

'I do apologise. I think my watch may be a little slow.'

Margaret immediately simpered, reaching up a hand to pat her iron-hard grey bob. I turned and was greeted with a warm handshake and a kiss on the cheek; I smelled Fahrenheit and a faint whiff of coconut – shampoo, perhaps? And then I stepped back and got my first proper look at Alexander. Only one word came to mind. Wow.

He was tall enough that I had to look up, although as I'm only five-foot-two that isn't hard. He was dressed smart-casual in blue jeans and a white shirt with a navy tie, with a tan leather jacket thrown over the top. I've always loved a man in blue jeans and a white shirt, and the ensemble showed his physique perfectly; he was strong without being stocky. A Mediterranean tan, startlingly green eyes and soft brown hair left becomingly longer on top completed the picture. I could well understand Margaret's uncharacteristic behaviour. I was glad I had worn the dress.

'Well, let's get going, shall we?' Margaret snapped. I realised I was staring like a schoolgirl with a crush.

I felt awkward standing outside the town hall, smiling my happiest 'I love teaching' smile, while Margaret glared at me from behind the photographer's shoulder. I was aware of the new guy's eyes on me the whole time, coolly appraising me. I glanced at him between false smiles, and he winked. I felt a heat in my belly that I hadn't felt around a man for a long time. He was truly gorgeous, a *GQ* model in the flesh. They should have picked him for the brochure; it would certainly have pulled the female students in.

The whole thing, thank heavens, took only about twenty minutes. I shifted from one foot to the other, realising I was waiting to see if he would speak. I wasn't disappointed. My heart dropped when Margaret invited him into the town hall for coffee, but he shook his head, instead turning and beaming at me.

'I was thinking of going to that new little Spanish restaurant across the road for an early lunch. Would you like to join me, Kelly?'

I grinned, noticing Margaret's mouth open in an 'oh' of surprise. I would no doubt pay for this at my next observation, but frankly I didn't care.

'I would love to, thank you.'

Margaret stalked off without a goodbye. Alexander offered me his arm and we crossed over the road, my hand resting lightly in the crook of his elbow. I felt as fluttery as a teenager, and told myself sharply to get a grip. No doubt he was already used to the girls in the office falling all over him; I wouldn't do myself any favours by acting like a giddy teenager. No, I decided, I would be cool and aloof. Kim would be proud.

'Thank you,' he murmured. I looked up, confused.

'For what?'

'Giving me an excuse to get out of spending any time with that dragon.' He nodded back towards where Margaret had disappeared into the building. Before I could feel insulted that he had only offered me lunch to get away from her, he added, '. . . though of course I would have invited you anyway.'

He was quite the gentleman, holding the door open for me and then pulling out my chair as I sat down. We ordered a tapas sharer and a bottle of white, with me trying to look knowledgeable when he commented on the vintage and chatted casually about work. He got up to go to the toilet before the food arrived, and I swiftly texted Kim.

Manager's bloody gorgeous. Doing lunch.

She texted back almost immediately: *Hussy*.

I was smiling at that when he returned and I placed my phone back in my pocket, feeling rude. He nodded at it as he sat down opposite me.

'Boyfriend?' he enquired, and I vehemently shook my head.

'Oh, no. I don't have the time; too overworked,' I quipped.

'Well, I'll have to see if I can do something with your schedule; we can't have our "face of Adult Ed" taking time off with stress, now, can we?'

I pulled a face at his sarcasm, but he had already changed the subject. He seemed to want to know everything about me, from where I went to school to my favourite food. His quizzing was so relentless that I had to wonder if he was really interested in me or if this was how the council carried out their criminal checks these days.

'What about you?' I asked, finally getting a question of my own in as I speared an olive. 'You haven't said much about yourself.'

'What do you want to know?'

He said the words easily, lightly, but I caught a brief look of wariness on his face. He seemed guarded: why? Especially after grilling me with questions. It didn't make sense.

'Well, there's very little to tell,' he said eventually. 'My father is Greek Cypriot; we have a property business over there. I went to Oxford . . .'

Oxford Uni? Another wow. I was proud enough of my degree from Warwick, which I had got into by the skin of my teeth, but he must be super-intelligent to have got into Oxford. Either that or Daddy had the right contacts.

'I enjoy skiing, not that I get the chance very often, and also horse riding.'

I smiled. Finally, something we had in common. Skiing was totally over my budget, but I've loved horse riding since I was a kid. I told him so, and was shocked by his next comment.

'I didn't really ride as a boy. It's something my wife introduced me to.'

Wife? I nearly choked on my chorizo. Typical: I was either completely wrong and he didn't fancy me at all or he was looking for an affair. I don't date married men. Never have, never will. I've fallen out with friends over this exact topic, in fact.

'You seem disappointed,' he observed, and I flushed with embarrassment.

'That's a little arrogant,' I snapped. He just smiled, leaning back in his chair and looking at me through narrowed eyes, both searching and amused.

'Am I wrong?'

'Absolutely.' I speared another olive with considerably

more force. 'It would be wholly inappropriate. You're my boss.'

'I am not; merely in a higher position. I have no direct dealings with the tutors. And I'm intrigued. Exactly what would be "wholly inappropriate"?'

That flustered me.

'What? Well . . . you . . . whatever you just meant,' I finished lamely.

He chuckled, a deep throaty sound that I would later come to recognise, and which would make things deep in my body instantly tighten.

'If it makes any difference, me and my wife are separated. The divorce is very close to being finalised. We married too young, ended up staying together for the sake of appearances more than anything. Typical story, I suppose.'

A dark shadow flitted across his face and then was gone, leaving the same easy smile and sexy glint to his eye. There was a great deal more to his story, that much was apparent.

I played him at his own game: 'Makes a difference to what, exactly?'

He chuckled again and leaned over the table towards me. I felt acutely aware of his proximity, the heat in my belly travelling to my face. I've always been a bit of a blusher, much to my chagrin.

'I would like to ask you out for dinner. You're very attractive, not to mention intriguing, and I'd like to get to know you better.'

The phrase 'get to know you better' hung in the air. He continued to gaze at me, only leaving my eyes to glance at my lips. I realised I was nipping my bottom lip with my teeth, something I only do when aroused. I excused myself without answering, reaching again for my phone as soon as I shut the ladies' door behind me.

Married.

Kim must have been literally staring at her phone as her reply came within seconds.

Bastard!

Not together though, getting divorced.

Yeah yeah. Be careful. He's still the boss.

I smiled ruefully. She was right, of course. I mentally squared my shoulders and headed back out. There were other men, other dates.

Not as hot as this one, my inner slut protested. I told her to shut up.

'I'm sorry,' I said firmly as I slid back into my seat, noticing his gaze brush across my legs, 'but I don't date married men. Divorcing or otherwise. It's just too complicated for me.'

'Ah. Well. I respect that.'

'Thank you.'

The exchange sounded very formal, and we sat in what I thought was an awkward silence until he broke it, looking at me intently.

'You know, you should wear red; it would suit you. It takes a beautiful woman to wear red.'

I was both pleased at the compliment and annoyed at his impromptu fashion advice, so I smiled politely and said nothing.

The awkward silence resumed. Tapas finished, I drained my wine glass.

'I must go, I have things to do,' I said, but as I stood up I felt reluctant to leave.

He shook my hand, refusing my offer to contribute to the cost of lunch, but there was no kiss on the cheek this time, and I was mentally kicking myself as I walked out of the restaurant. I couldn't resist a look back to see if he was watching, but felt a stab of jealousy to see him talking to the young blonde waitress. Most likely just paying the bill, but nevertheless I stomped off, hands in my pockets and face buried in my coat against the wind.

I was due to visit my mother, something else I wasn't look-ing forward to, as spending time with her was generally as fun as pulling teeth, but she was in an unexpected good mood. I took the hot chocolate she offered me grate-fully, kneeling on the floor in front of the fire. As usual the house was immaculate, as was she. I wondered if she had ever been tempted by an unsuitable man, though I couldn't imagine her ever being tempted by anything. She had been beautiful once – old family photos showed a sparklingly pretty young woman, all eighties blonde waves and bleached jeans hugging a great figure – but there was a bitter look to her face now, as if life had given her lemons that were too sour for lemonade.

'How did the photo thing go?' she asked, sitting at the table and passing me a coaster for the hot chocolate – God forbid I should put it down on the mantelpiece without one.

'OK,' I shrugged, contemplating telling her about lunch. Instead I asked her straight out: 'Ever been out with someone you shouldn't? Before Dad, I mean?'

She looked surprised, then smirked.

'Why, have you met someone?'

'Well, I wouldn't go that far . . .' I told her about lunch with Alexander, and his offer of taking me out, and the revelation about his divorce.

She thought for a minute.

'You're not getting any younger. I'd take what I could get, if I were you.'

'Mum, I'm twenty-six!' I protested.

'Yes, and already divorced once. You'll be like that Bridget Jones woman, you mark my words.'

'Thank you so much for those pearls of wisdom,' I huffed into my chocolate.

Ten minutes with my mother and I had gone from feeling sexy and desirable – if a little confused – to frumpy and past it. Somehow she always managed to leave me doubting myself. No matter how hard I had worked at school or what I had achieved, it had never been enough to gain her approval. I had pretty much given up trying. I knew what she wanted from me: a good marriage, to a man with money, and some well-behaved grandkids she could trot out in front of the relatives. Where her old-fashioned attitudes came from I had never been able to work out, but I certainly wasn't in the mood for being made to feel like an old spinster. Or even like Bridget Jones.

I was still annoyed when I got home, and nearly ignored the ringing of the doorbell when I heard it. I wrenched it open, my glare causing the delivery boy to step back in surprise.

'Er . . . Miss Lawrence?'

I stared at the huge bouquet of lilies in his hand. Even

as I signed for them, I had a feeling they were from *him*, but I told myself not to be so stupid.

But my intuition was right. I picked the little embossed card out of the flowers. Sure enough, it read: *Pick you up at eight. Wear red. Alex.*

Just like that.

Chapter Three

'You're not wearing red.'

He had arrived at my door, at exactly eight o'clock, looking good enough to eat in chinos and a pale blue shirt. He frowned at my dress.

'It's blue.'

I smirked. 'Very perceptive, aren't you?'

In truth, I had initially changed into a red bodycon that I knew would wow him, and then discarded it in favour of a dark blue shift dress with impressive cleavage. I hate being told what to do, and didn't want to appear too eager; the fact that I was allowing him to pick me up at all was bad enough. I had spent a good hour arguing with myself over it, then finally decided: what the hell? It was only a date. But I was damned if I was letting a man tell me what to wear, no matter how hot he might happen to be.

'It's very nice,' he conceded, holding open the car door. He drove a Mercedes, which somehow fit.

'Thank you.'

'Red would have been better.'

I shook my head in exasperation as I did my best to slide into the car without flashing my knickers.

'Are you always so . . . dominant?'

At that, he turned and looked at me with a gaze so steamy I felt that tightening low in my belly . . . and lower places still.

'Yes,' he said firmly. His next words made my breath stop: 'I've a good mind to put you over my knee.'

My mouth went dry; right then it sounded like a deliciously wicked idea. I glanced at his strong hands involuntarily. He noticed my gaze and smiled, then turned to start the car, breaking the moment. I clipped in the seatbelt.

'I thought Prague first?'

Prague was a fancy wine bar on the 'nicer' side of town. I sometimes drank in there with Kimberly, though the cocktails were far pricier than either of us could really afford.

'Sounds great,' I nodded.

We fell into silence as he drove, and I shifted uncomfortably in my seat.

'Are you warm enough?'

He turned on the heating and the seat, too, warmed against my bare thighs. Tights would have been a good idea, but I hadn't been able to find a pair that weren't laddered or bobbly, and stockings seemed too sexy for a first date.

'Nice,' I commented on the seats, shifting over the leather.

'Indeed,' he murmured, gazing directly at my thighs where my skirt had lifted slightly with my movement, his eyes following my vine tattoo from my knee to where it disappeared beneath my dress.

I blushed, yet again, and was glad of the dark. What the hell was wrong with me around this man? I was glad when we reached town; the nearness of him had seemed to grow more intense as we drove, the heat from the leather beneath me warming parts I was trying not to think about. I stepped out into the cool air gratefully, hugging my coat around me. He offered me his arm, and I hesitated but then took it. It wasn't the time to come over all feminist, not in five-inch spike-heeled shoes.

He ordered two red wines without asking what I wanted, and I frowned at him.

'You said at lunch you liked red wine,' he said evenly, and I felt slightly silly. So he had asked me to wear red – so what? It didn't mean he was some kind of control freak; he probably just liked the colour. But as he guided me to a chair I had to admit to feeling somewhat unnerved; there was the fact that I hadn't given him my address to pick me up or send the flowers in the first place, which meant he had gone into the work files to look it up. Which he was perfectly allowed to do, I suppose, but it was more than a little presumptuous, wasn't it? And he had just turned up at eight, as if it had never occurred to him that I might not actually want to go out.

I asked him that very question as we sat down: 'What if you had knocked my door and I had told you no?'

He looked straight into my eyes, his expression unreadable.

'But you didn't, did you?'

And I had no answer.

*

The night turned to small talk. I was shyer than I had been at lunch, the red wine for once not making me brave. He switched to Coke after the first drink, while I guzzled my way through a bottle of Merlot. At one point I noticed him watch me as I swallowed, his eyes travelling down my throat as if he could see the liquid going down. It was surprisingly sexual. I was starting to feel braver – and more than a little tipsy – when he stood and again offered me his arm.

'Shall we go? I have quite an early start.'

I was disappointed, having hoped to go for dinner, or even clubbing. I would have loved to see Mr Dominant let his hair down, I giggled to myself, nearly tripping over my heels. I was far from drunk but in that merry state when things seem so much funnier, and I was still giggling as he led me back to the car. He shook his head in bemusement.

'You're delightful to spend time with,' he commented.

'Why, thank you, Sir.'

His eyes darkened with something I couldn't quite read, and the look he turned on me was pure sex.

'Oh, but you will call me Sir,' he breathed.

I felt suddenly very sober, and very excited.

Again, he didn't speak on the way back to my apartment, and I was almost squirming with anticipation by the time he carefully parked the car. But there was no awkward sitting in silence while he waited to see if I would invite him in or while I waited for him to kiss me; he took it for granted that he was coming in. Getting out of the car and opening my door for me, he led me up the steps with one hand on the small of my back. I paused before I put the key in the lock, turning to him.

'Is this where I invite you in for coffee?' I quipped.

He practically growled at me.

'I don't want coffee,' he said, his eyes travelling down the length of my body.

I was shuddering with more than just cold as I let him in. Flustered, my heart pounded in anticipation – was he going to kiss me? And a hundred other questions flooded through my mind: did he want to sleep with me? Did I want to sleep with him? No, that was a stupid one; *was* I going to sleep with him? I busied myself turning on the light and kicking my cat, Tammy, into the kitchen. She eyed Alex with disapproval. When I turned round he was already seated, his gaze fixed on me.

'Take off the dress.'

I blinked rapidly, uncertain if I had heard him correctly. 'What?'

'You heard what I said. Take off the dress.'

I had no witty comeback or snappy retort; I wanted to do as he said. My hands fumbled at my zip – thankfully it was on the side – and I let my dress fall, pushing it down over my hips, and then stepping out of it awkwardly. I had never felt so exposed. Even though I was confident about my body – well, mostly, we all have hang-ups – and was no stranger to going topless at the beach, I felt unbearably naked in my lacy black bra and French knickers. I stood squirming with embarrassment as his eyes lazily took in every inch of me.

'What do you—?' I began, but he silenced me with an abrupt, 'Be quiet. Let me look at you.'

I stood there for what felt like hours, though of course it could only have been a few minutes, while he continued to drink me in with his gaze. I was a quivery mess, my breath shallow and my face once again flushed, and I could feel the wetness pooling between my legs, but he looked completely composed, only his eyes showing the heat of desire, and even that was controlled. Somehow his composure only made me feel more exposed – and more turned on.

'Come here,' he ordered. I started to walk towards him, swaying on my heels. As I reached him he lifted his hands up to my hips, trailing one hand along the vine and butterfly tattoo that snakes down from my pubic bone to my right knee.

'This is very pretty. I love the way it follows your curves.'

He traced his fingers back up to where the design stopped, just above my panties.

'Thank you,' I said, breath ragged.

He stared at me for an agonising time, then suddenly pulled me forward and twisted me so that I was over his knee, steadying myself on the floor in front of me with my hands.

'What the hell are you doing?!' I protested, but in spite of my consternation I didn't move, and as his hands moved over my ass cheeks, squeezing and caressing, my pussy throbbed in response. My body welcomed the touch of his fingers brushing over my crotch, even as my head spun at the bizarre situation I had found myself in.

'I told you you were going over my knee, didn't I?'

I sucked my breath in sharply. The blood rushing to my head as I dangled over his lap was only heightening my sensation.

'Didn't I?' he demanded, and without warning gave my ass a sharp slap.

I yelped in surprise, and he rubbed the offended area as if to soothe, before slapping it again. Although it stung, I felt a rush between my legs that was more pleasure than pain. The unfamiliarity of it added to the thrill.

'Yes,' I mumbled, fighting the urge to turn my ass up into his hand, which was again kneading away. My embarrassment at being upended over his knee was only turning me on all the more.

'Yes what?'

Another slap, harder this time. For a minute I didn't understand what he meant, and then as I realised I burned with frustration, writhing away, but he pinned me down easily. The sense of being helpless under his hands added as much to my desire as it did to my frustration.

'Yes what?'

'Sir,' I said sulkily. 'Yes, Sir.'

He chuckled that dark laugh again, patting my ass approvingly.

'Good girl.'

Then with one hand he wrenched my knickers down to my knees, exposing my ass and pussy to the air and to his gaze. My clit and nipples were throbbing, the inside of my vagina tightening, and as much as part of me wanted to jump out of his grasp and demand he leave, my body was a purring kitten under his touch; she wasn't going anywhere. My inner slut was well and truly taking over.

He slipped a finger inside me.

'You're wet,' he stated, then slapped me again. 'You dirty bitch.'

I moaned audibly, and he started spanking me in earnest then, using the flat of his hand across both cheeks, every so often pausing for a soothing rub before resuming the punishment. I was moaning and writhing like a bitch in heat, feeling my own juices running down my legs. My ass was burning; his slaps were only just the right side of pain. Finally he stopped, leaving me a sweaty, trembling mess, and brushed his fingers across my pussy, which was now soaking and aching to be touched. He began to circle my clit expertly with one fingertip, and I was moving my hips against his hands, desperate for the release I could feel building.

'Come for me, bitch,' he commanded – and I did, in a rush of liquid that soaked his hands and my thighs, with an unsuppressed scream.

I lay there for a few minutes, panting, before he gently helped me up. I collapsed on to the settee, shocked. I had never climaxed so easily with a man, and certainly not on the first day of meeting him, or from so little stimulation. One fingertip? Wow.

I reached for him, whether wanting more sex or comfort I didn't know, but he was standing up and straightening his clothes.

'You will wear red next time.'

And he left, leaving me stunned.

Journal extract

Crazy. He's crazy. To be so . . . intense, and then just get up and leave? I mean, I don't know what to think now. Should I be insulted or not?

I knew there was something off about him. You would think I'd know to listen to my instincts by now. As if him being my boss wasn't bad enough! He turns out to be a kinky bastard too!

Worst of it is, I enjoyed it. Way too much. I've never been so turned on in my life. I think he could have asked me to do just about anything and I would have gone along with it. How wrong is that?

Chapter Four

I wasn't going to see him again. Honestly, I had every intention of never speaking to the guy again. The whole next day I felt mortified, flushing with embarrassment every time I remembered the sensation of being over his knee, of coming over his hand. The rush of desire the memory gave me made the mortification worse. How could I be turned on by having him disrespect me like that? But then: had he, really? He had been nothing but courteous all night, and I had let him spank me; other than a few half-hearted protestations, I had made no real effort to ask him to stop. I wrestled with it for the rest of the weekend, not even confiding in Kimberly.

In spite of my final decision to leave him well alone, I still went to bed on Sunday night feeling disgruntled that he hadn't been in touch. It was just plain rude. I couldn't get my head around the way he had upped and left, or his parting shot: 'You will wear red next time.' That implied he wanted to see me again, surely?

I lay in bed that night trying not to think about him, and the things he had done, but typically the more I tried to fight the thoughts the more tenacious they were. Eventually, in an attempt to get it out of my system, I slipped my hand down between my legs and brought myself to a quick orgasm, again picturing myself tipped over his knee while he punished me, imagining those hands between my legs, then moaning in frustration when my administrations failed to satisfy me completely.

I dragged myself out of bed on Monday morning, reluctant as always to begin the week, and showered and dressed quickly. My body still felt acutely sensitive; Alex sprang into my head unbidden as I ran my soaped hands over my breasts. Frankly, it was getting annoying.

In a rush to leave the house, as always, I threw my lesson plans and other bits and pieces into my bag. That was when my phone beeped.

I've been thinking about you. Would you like to do lunch? Alex.

I glared at the screen even as my heart leapt, and the stubborn teenage rebel in me reared her pretty head. Although there were better reasons for me to refuse, not least the bizarre spanking incident, my reply had more to do with me stamping my feet at his cocky attitude than anything else.

No, very busy. Sorry.

I waited for a reply, perhaps hoping he would try to talk me round, but there was nothing. I hoisted my bag on my shoulder and ran for the bus. The morning crawled by; I checked my phone every ten minutes, for what I don't know. I had turned him down and quite bluntly, too, but then, I had tried to turn him down for Saturday night and been rewarded with flowers. I shifted on my seat; my ass was still sore, which only provided with each twinge of pain an accompanying stab of remembered pleasure.

I was fractious and distracted with my students, who regarded me warily, used to my usual sunny-if-scatter-brained self. At lunch I reached for my phone, wondering if it was too late to change my mind, when Amanda came in, overly jolly as usual, waving papers at me.

'I noticed you still haven't put last week's attendance figures in, Kelly.'

In spite of her jolly demeanour there was a hint of annoyance in her voice that I knew meant she was pretty pissed off. It wouldn't be the first time she had to chase me – or the other tutors for that matter – for attendance figures. Manually entering each class's data every month wasn't high on anyone's to-do list.

I started to search for a better excuse than 'I forgot' but she had already pulled up a chair and sat down, spreading out a register in front of me.

'. . . so I thought we'd go through them together the old-fashioned way, and as you're obviously having trouble doing them electronically, I've booked you in for an hour's training after work next week. We like to give all our tutors as much support as we can.'

She beamed at me, pleased with herself. What the hell did she want, a medal? I wasn't getting away this dinner-time, that was for sure. And, as if on cue, my phone beeped again.

Still busy?

Amanda looked at my phone pointedly as I picked up to reply, firing off *Yes. Just been collared by line manager*, and then wondered if I should put a kiss or not. Which was ridiculous, when just a few hours ago I had been resolving never to talk to the man again. This is why I hate text messages, I mused. Although I use them frequently, they're a tricky way to communicate, because you can only get the basic message across. There's no tone of voice, so it's easy to take an innocent comment in a totally different way than how the author intended. I sat debating with myself until Amanda cleared her throat in annoyance, then in a hurry I put a whole row of kisses and pressed 'send' before I realised quite what I was doing.

All afternoon I received no reply. By the time I had finished work and managed to escape before either Amanda or Margaret found something else for me to do, I had gone back to the opinion that he was an obnoxious idiot. The fact that he was probably busy himself carried no weight with me; I was both intrigued and outraged by his behaviour on Saturday and needed some kind of explanation, at least.

I was still thinking about him on the way home, the frustration making me walk twice as fast as usual. Then, as I passed Shane's tattoo parlour, its lit window bright against the dark street, I had my answer: perhaps I just needed a good shag. It had been a few weeks, and the events of the weekend had wound me up sexually; I needed some release. I turned back and went into Deviant Art, Shane's shop, hoping he wasn't busy, and not quite sure how I would be received. I hadn't seen him in a couple of weeks, in an attempt to bring our friendship back to a platonic level. Heading into the shop now would undo all of that, but for the moment I didn't mind one bit. After all, wasn't it for

times like these that you could call on a 'friend with benefits'? A part of me felt bad for using him like this, but we'd
both signed up to this, and he was an old friend. I would
invite him round and get rid of my frustration, which
would, hopefully, stop me from obsessing about Alex.

Shane looked up as I entered, causing the bell to ring.
He had the reception area decorated beautifully, all pinks
and purples and gothic and Japanese art. Shane took
his profession seriously and his place of business is a far
cry from the stereotypical dingy backstreet tattoo shop.
Unfortunately for a lot of his customers, there was no six-
foot-tall heavily tattooed hot chick wandering around;
reality TV shows have a lot to answer for. He smiled at
me, tucking his long hair behind one ear. Unlike the shop,
Shane does look like the stereotype. Heavily tattooed and
muscled, with that whole American rockabilly look going
on, his sweet personality often comes as a surprise to people who don't know him very well.

'Hey stranger. Been busy?'

'Very. So I was wondering—'

'If I'm free tonight?' he grinned, then shook his head
and tapped the appointment book in front of him.

'Wish I was, babe, but I've got a late one. Won't be
done till around ten, and I know you're a lightweight who
needs her beauty sleep. How's tomorrow?'

I sighed. Tomorrow would be great for a catch-up, but
I was horny *now*. I shocked myself with my next actions, as
I leaned over the desk, my lips close to his.

'How's right now?'

I tipped my head towards the back room. His eyes widened, then he closed the gap and kissed me softly.

I responded eagerly, almost hungrily, nipping his bottom lip with my teeth. I immediately thought about Alex; he hadn't even kissed me. He had seen me naked and given me an orgasm, yet he hadn't even kissed me. Wasn't that weird? I pushed the thought away and kissed Shane harder. Grabbing my hand, he pulled me into the back room, closing the door behind us. He was eager, pulling at me with hot hands, but his smile was bemused.

'What's got into you?'

'I just need to,' I said honestly.

He frowned as if he was going to say something, then thought better of it and pulled me over to the couch, his hands in my hair and on the small of my back, pulling me into him. I was already pulling at his zip, in no mood for too much kissing and smooching; I wanted him inside me. Freeing his zip, I went down on my knees, hearing him gasp in surprise at my forwardness. He was already hard when I took him into my mouth, but even as I tried to throw myself into the moment I was thinking about Alex. How would he react if I went on my knees for him? How his cock might feel in my mouth . . . I swirled my tongue around the tip, smiling when it twitched eagerly, and slid my mouth as far down as I could take him. He's big, so it was a challenge, but I sucked on him greedily, my thoughts all with Alex still, wondering how big he was, how he would taste. I moaned when I felt Shane tug at my hair and took him that bit deeper.

'Babe . . .' Shane was pulling me up gently. 'Slow down, or I won't last long.'

'It's OK.'

I was after instant gratification, not a long, drawn-out session.

I moved round so I was sitting on the edge of the couch, reaching for him. I was ready, and I pulled him in between my parted legs. I would hang my head in shame later, but right then the inner slut was well and truly in control, and Shane was there, and willing.

'Fuck me,' I demanded.

He needed no further prompting, lifting my skirt up around my thighs and teasing me through my knickers, before slipping them to the side and sliding into me. I contracted round him, instinctively rocking my hips in time with his, pulling him closer with my thighs. I could worry about the sudden display of wantonness later, but right now I just wanted him to fuck me, to give me the release I had needed since Alex had put me over his knee on Saturday night.

It didn't happen. Shane preferred a lighter touch; in spite of his edgy looks he was a gentleman, even his work with the needle was delicate, and while I usually appreciated his tender approach, it wasn't what I wanted right now. As I urged him on I felt frustrated; it wasn't enough. I wanted the almost illicit excitement I had felt with Alex, the dirty talk and the feeling of being totally in his power. The need I had felt, pinned to his knees, my pussy and ass exposed to his gaze while I writhed on him like a cat. Shane, bless him, just couldn't inspire that in me.

As he had warned, he climaxed quickly, shuddering against me. He buried his face in my neck and I patted his back almost awkwardly. He stayed here, his breath hot on my neck, until I grew uncomfortable and had to pull away. He stepped back and regarded me with a lazy appreciation.

'That was amazing, you little tiger. Hard day at work?'

I laughed, sliding off the couch and readjusting my knickers, which were damp and twisted up around the side of my ass; I felt like a teenager again, sneaking a fumble with my first boyfriend.

'Something like that.'

'So, we still on for tomorrow? Film and a beer, maybe? I've got some good DVDs I can bring round.'

I paused, noticed his face drop, and then nodded quickly.

'Of course. We need a good catch-up.'

He winked at that and I felt guilty. Walking home, leaving Shane dazed but happy at our impromptu afternoon tryst, I was upset at my behaviour. Shane was, sex aside, one of my best friends and I knew he thought a lot of me, as I did of him. I hated the idea that I had just used him when, if I had the courage to admit it, I'd really wanted Alex. Shane didn't deserve that, and I was mentally flagellating myself when I heard my phone going off in my bag. I was expecting it to be Shane, and so I didn't look at the screen when I answered it – to a very different voice altogether.

'Kelly. It's Alex. As we couldn't get together today, how's tomorrow evening?'

No hello, no apologies, just that abrupt, arrogant tone of voice. That was, as much as I hated to admit it, sexy as hell.

Too shocked to form a coherent answer I mumbled something non-committal and he went on, his voice softer: 'I'd like to explain about Saturday.'

Finally. I tried to muster some dignity and managed to answer him coolly.

'I'd appreciate that, yes.'

'Good. If it's all right to come to yours, I'll be there about seven?'

I gave him my assent and as he hung up I was beaming. Only then did I remember I had just arranged to see Shane the following night; I could hardly cancel after the way I had just thrown myself at him.

But I knew I would.

Journal extract

I can't see him again; he's going to drive me crazy. And if he was like that on a first date what the hell is he going to want to do on a second? But then he did say he wanted to explain, didn't he? And I want to know what he's got to say.

Or do I just want to see him? He's so sexy, just hearing his voice on the phone made me gooey. It's hardly a good thing, though, when I don't know what to expect from him. And he's so bossy.

I just feel like I can't control how this Alex guy affects me, and I don't like that, it's scary. But . . . I do want to see him.

Chapter Five

I was panicking, spring-cleaning my flat and trying on outfit after outfit. Our second date was looming and, with less than half an hour to go, I was a butterfly jar of nerves. Not to mention wrestling with that age-old question: what to wear? I remembered his insistence on me wearing red, and went backwards and forwards between wanting him to think I looked nice and refusing to let him think he could tell me what to do.

I acquiesced in the end, going for my favourite jeans that hugged my ass and a red top with a plunging V-neck. I would have preferred a more impressive cleavage to put into it, but a push-up bra did the trick. I was determined he wasn't going to be seeing my underwear again – not that night, anyway.

I was oscillating between so many different emotions that I poured myself a glass of wine while I waited. As the clock ticked towards seven I thought about the fact that I hadn't heard from him all day and began to torture myself with thoughts of him changing his mind and not turning up at all.

When the doorbell went, at exactly seven o'clock, I flew out of my seat at once, before composing myself and giving my reflection the once-over. I had chosen deep red lipstick to match the top, but had gnawed most of it off with nerves, and had to quickly wipe it off my teeth with my finger.

I aimed for a calm, only mildly interested expression as I opened the door, but straight away felt myself going as red as my outfit.

'You look lovely.'

'Thank you.'

'I told you that was your colour, didn't I? I'm glad you decided to stop being stubborn.'

I glared at him, embarrassment forgotten, as I stepped aside so he could enter. Only then did I notice the small package he was holding: a carefully wrapped gift that he put into my hands but then covered with his own before I could tear the wrapping off. I loved presents.

'Please. I want you to open it after I've gone. You'll understand better then.'

Understand what? I was intrigued, a sensation I was fast becoming used to where Alex was concerned. I placed the gift on the dresser and as he crossed over to sit down, a flashback of what we did on that sofa the last time he was here had my face colouring again. I was going to have to invest in some heavy-duty foundation, or learn to stop blushing.

We made idle chit-chat about our respective workdays as I busied myself pouring him a glass of wine, but I was barely listening, until I caught something that stopped me in my tracks.

'. . . for a couple of weeks at least.'

'You're going away?'

I hated how distraught I sounded, especially when he smiled at my concern.

'Yes, Dad's not getting any younger and he needs my help on a few business matters. I may well be relocating to Cyprus permanently, but not for a few years yet. But yes, I fly out tomorrow.'

I sat down next to him, unsure how to take this latest bit of news. That stopped any fledgling romance in its tracks, surely? But he hadn't come round to tell me this – and indeed, why should he? As if reading my mind, he put down his glass and cleared his throat.

'So, about the other night . . .'

I waited, unable to meet his eyes again, my gaze dropping instead to his hands, the same hands that had 'punished' me with such expertise. In spite of his managerial office job they were workman's hands, olive and gnarly, with those thick fingers that had so confidently kneaded my ass. They didn't match his suave demeanour, those hands. I was glad to note they were not manicured. I'm not a fan of the current New Man trend – your boyfriend not just borrowing your moisturiser but having his own. I like men to be men.

'I realise it must have seemed somewhat bizarre to you.'

'Just a bit.'

That was quite possibly the understatement of the year.

He ran his hand through his hair, looking flustered for the first time since I had met him. I had noticed, too, the way he spoke very formally at times, almost guardedly, and I didn't think that quirk of speech was just down to his

parents not being English, or the middle-class upbringing
he had clearly had. He was someone who obviously liked
to be in control, so this nervous gesture made me warm
to him. Whatever it was he wanted to say, I was pleased to
note that, for the first time, he seemed concerned about
my reaction.

'I'm assuming you've heard of BDSM practices?'

I raised my eyebrows.

'As in kinky sex? Bondage and things? Yes, of course.'

He looked relieved, then worried again when I went
on: 'But it's not something I'm familiar with.'

He took a deep breath, inching closer to me, and looked
into my eyes with that intense gaze of his.

'OK. Well, I *am* familiar with it; very familiar in fact.
I'm what is usually known as a dominant, meaning that in
a relationship I expect my partner to be sexually submissive to me, much like you experienced the other night. I'd
like to carry on dating you, Kelly, so I suppose what I'm
trying to ask you is whether or not you would be happy to
explore that with me?'

As much as my poor brain was screaming warnings at
me, I was beaming that he had mentioned we were 'dating'.
It took me a few seconds to catch up with what else he had
told me. A dominant? What the hell did that mean? He
was going to want to spank me on a regular basis? I could
live with that.

'Well, how far does this BDSM stuff go? I mean, I like
to think I'm adventurous but this is all new to me.'

'You enjoyed being bent over my knee.'

A statement, not a question. Remembering how I had
writhed on his lap and soaked his thighs and hand with my

43

juices, I could hardly pretend otherwise. But the way he had just walked out afterwards still rankled. After such an intimate, boundary-pushing moment, I had needed comfort, and had felt bereft at his rude departure.

'You just left,' I said accusingly. 'I didn't know what to think.'

I didn't know how to convey how vulnerable he had made me feel.

'I've never done anything like that before,' I said instead, looking down at my hands, which were twisting nervously in my lap.

He looked contrite, and his next words surprised me.

'I'm sorry. Really. I never wanted to upset you. I was quite annoyed with myself for showing my hand so soon, not to mention stupidly turned on. I didn't want to go any further and leave you full of regrets. Am I forgiven?'

Forgiven. It seemed an odd choice of word, but then the whole situation was odd, to say the least. The conversation was surreal, as if it was happening to somebody else and I was merely listening in. He sounded so formal, too, as if we were discussing work, and I remembered with a rush of embarrassment just who he was. How would I ever face him if I saw him at a work function, having been over his knee? Still, I tried not to let my anxiety show as I put my best 'teacher' voice on.

'Just don't do it again.'

I was aiming to sound stern, pull my independent-woman, I-don't-take-any-shit face, but inside I was giving myself a mental high-five at his admittance of being 'stupidly turned on'. It hadn't just been me, then.

I was finding it hard to digest the information he'd just

presented me with. I had guessed as much – that he had a sexual kink; after all, bending your new date over your knee is hardly common behaviour – but this frank admission, and offer, I hadn't expected.

'What exactly would it entail, being your submissive? What would I do?'

'It basically involves you – as the name implies – submitting to my desires in bed, letting me call the shots, if you like. It would be up to you how far we go. There are different practices, like spanking, for example, and we can explore whichever ones you like.'

His eyes hinted at unspoken desires.

'There are a few things I have in mind. Of course, I'd respect your boundaries. Though they would change over time.'

Boundaries. I thought of my slutty behaviour with Shane; Alex had already redefined my boundaries, more than he knew. I didn't know what to say to him. I wanted to carry on seeing him, yes, and any concerns I had over his impending divorce and his work status had faded into the background compared to this new revelation, but I had no real idea what I would be agreeing to. I couldn't lie to myself: I was intrigued. I wanted to know exactly what he had in mind, to experience the secrets his words hinted at. The old restlessness I always felt in sexual relationships had reared its head, but for a different reason; Alex seemed to be offering something that might just satisfy it. Still, I was too wary to just throw myself head-first into a situation I didn't understand with a man I barely knew.

'I want to see you again, I think. But I can't agree to this; I don't even fully understand it.'

'Of course. I expected you to say that. Which is why my going away has perhaps come at a good time. Use the next couple of weeks to do some research, explore your feelings, make your mind up, and you can give me an answer when I get back.'

That made sense, though I had no idea what he meant by research – like I was going to walk into my local library and ask for books on bondage?

I hated the fact that he was going away, and hated that I hated it, but it might give me some clarity. Really, I knew I should be keeping well away from this man, but I just didn't want to.

'OK,' I agreed, 'I'll do that. But I can't tell you now how I'll feel about things by the time you get back. This isn't something I've ever even considered before.'

'Yet you didn't complain on Saturday night. My judgments are usually good, Kelly, and I believe this is something that's in you, too.'

Well, that surprised me. Had I given off some phero-mone I was unaware of? Please, spank me? But he was right: I hadn't complained any more than Shane had when I all but dragged him on to his couch. Something in me had responded to Alex, whether I liked it or not.

I was thinking it all over, my head whirling, when he drained his glass and stood up.

'I really do need to go; I've got an early start for the airport. I hope we can pick this up where we left off.'

I stood up and walked him to the door, bemused. Of all the scenarios I had been expecting, this was not one of them. I felt a surge of disappointment that he hadn't so much as tried to touch me, and now he was going away. I realised that, in spite of my earlier insistence to myself, I had expected – hell, I had probably hoped for – a repeat of Saturday, or better yet a continuation of it. And here he was dropping some crazy shit on me and then just walking out. Again. It seemed to be a habit of his, and not one I liked.

'You haven't even kissed me,' I blurted out at the door.

Alex turned to me, his eyes searching my face, but he didn't answer or respond, just looked at me until I had to elaborate.

'I mean, we've been out on a date, done . . . some stuff, and now you come and ask me this, and you haven't even tried to kiss me.'

The wicked look on his face was back, his eyes narrowing as he looked me up and down, gaze lingering on my cleavage, then my lips. The way he could switch from being the perfect gentleman to looking at me like he could strip my clothes from my flesh with just the force of his gaze made my mouth go dry.

'Do you want me to kiss you?'

His voice was soft, low, but completely self-assured. I nodded.

'Yes.'

'Yes what?'

This again. I shook my head in protest at his insistence on this game, even as the words came out.

'Yes . . . Sir.'

He stepped towards me and took my head in his hands, roughly, lowering his mouth to mine. He passed his lips over mine in light movements, down my chin and across my neck up to my ear, his hands holding my head still while he nipped at my earlobe, then again moved his mouth across my skin, only just touching his lips against my flesh until he was back at my waiting mouth. He hesitated for just a moment, looking from my lips to my eyes and back, before gripping the back of my neck tightly and all but crushing his mouth on to mine.

I've never liked kisses with too much tongue, yet a thrill went through me as he held my face immobile in his hands, stretched open my mouth with his own, and slid his tongue deep inside me, invading me as if my throat were a new territory to be conquered. When he let me go I was gasping.

'That better?'

He looked at me as if he was mocking me, yet I sensed a need behind the words, and for more than just sex. If it was for approval, he had it.

'Yes.'

'You liked it?'

'Yes.'

'Good. Because that's how I like to fuck.'

He left then, giving me a little wave as he reached his car, leaving me with a pool of wetness between my legs and my face burning. I went back inside, the night's revelations weighing heavy on my mind. It was high time I confided in Kimberly, and not least because I was going to need her help with my 'research'.

It was only as I reached for the phone that I remembered his gift, and I unwrapped it with shaky fingers, smiling to myself when the wrapping paper fell away to reveal a pink and black silk blindfold. What else had I expected? But when I unfolded the mask I found two other objects:

tiny plastic butterflies with jewels dangling from them. I thought they were earrings at first, until closer inspection showed me the tiny clamps on the back.

'Nipple clamps,' Kimberly informed me the next day. 'They're nipple clamps. You put them on your boobs . . .'

'Yes, I get that, I know what you do with them.'

Not that I had ever used anything like them before. Wouldn't it just hurt? I have ultra-sensitive nipples, so I wasn't convinced that putting clamps on them would be pleasurable.

Going for the hands-on approach, Kim hoisted her top up and clipped one of the clamps to her bra. She yelped with pain as the clamp closed around her nipple and yanked it off, which of course made her yelp even louder. I burst into horrified giggles.

'Babe! I don't think you're supposed to use them like that.'

Kim rubbed her chest, wincing.

'You may as well stick pegs on your boobs. They're pretty, though.'

I held the other clamp up to the light, admiring it. They were deceptively pretty and harmless-looking. A bit like Alex.

I was still examining them when she turned a serious face to me.

'So what are you going to do?'

To that, I had no answer.

Journal extract

I still don't know what I'm going to do. I hardly know the guy, and it's not as if he's just asked me to consider dating him, or even sleeping with him on a regular basis; he's asking me to get involved in some kinky sex thing and I'm not sure I'm up for that.

Looked on internet with Kim and found out some pretty scary stuff. I don't really know how much he's into all this. I don't like pain, I know that much, but that whole dominant thing he does really turns me on. I've always preferred the guy to be in control so maybe he's right and it is something I'd take to. I'm young, free and single, after all, it's not as if I have to commit myself to anything, is it?

I told Shane I'd met someone – even though I don't know if that's the case – and he took it OK, looked a bit disappointed but there was no drama.

Went to the gym after work and ended up on the cross-trainer for double the time; trying to clear my head, I think. But I'm no closer to deciding anything. And I've hardly heard from Alex, just a few texts to say he's having a good trip; he hasn't mentioned his proposition. I can't work out if he's just playing games with me. But maybe that's the point.

Kim had this great idea – she's found a fetish club near town. We could go and check it out, get a feel for the scene. I can't do that on Google. It'll be a chance to dress up, if nothing else . . .

Chapter Six

'Well, it's certainly given us a chance to dress up.'

Kim unknowingly echoed my earlier thoughts. It was the following Friday, a mild evening after the first day of sunshine we'd had that year, and we were prancing around my flat admiring each other's outfits. I was dolled up to the nines in black PVC leggings and a corset top, with a velvet choker round my neck, but I wasn't sure if I looked more goth than kinky. Kim had bought thigh-high PVC boots especially for the occasion and couldn't walk in them; she was staggering around my flat trying to get drinks, wobbling precariously on her spiked heels. I had already downed two glasses of wine in an attempt to cure my nerves and was full of Dutch courage. We had phoned ahead, and the woman on the phone had sounded very middle-class, very professional. Not what I had been expecting, but then I didn't know just what I was expecting.

Going by the pictures on the Club Elite website, it was a pretty classy place, not the seedy dungeon I had antici-pated – or not just that, at any rate. The digital picture tour showed a homely chill-out room with a roaring log fire and sumptuous rugs and couches; the dance room and bar was very chic, like I imagined a Manhattan cocktail bar to be. (Having never been to Manhattan, my preconceptions were pretty much based on box sets of *Sex and the City*.) There was a spa, which had made Kimberly squeal with delight, and rows of very clinical-looking lockers and changing rooms.

I had been feeling disappointed with the lack of kink until a picture of the 'playroom' flashed up. At first it looked like another beautifully decorated room, with a few nude statues and some erotic art on the walls, until we took a closer look at the 'furniture'. Leather crosses with cuffs, black vinyl couches with some strange-looking attachments, and even a zebra-print sex swing that admittedly perked my interest. There were also a couple of bedrooms, one in pink and purple silk and velvet with a gorgeous four-poster, the other with a scary-looking black metal bed with handcuffs attached. Nothing appeared too 'out there', but my mind boggled as to what exactly went on inside. The voice on the phone had assured me it was a fetish club, not a sex club or swingers' club, and I hadn't had the nerve to tell her I didn't know the difference between any of them.

'Swingers' clubs,' Kim had informed me, 'are full of middle-aged, middle-class people having sex all over the place.'

'How do you know?'

'Saw it on a documentary.' As if that was the last word on the matter.

So there we were, all dressed up and ready to go. Kim was driving, and we had a childishly funny moment entering 'kinky sex club' into her satnav system before settling down and finding the correct route. I was quiet as we drove through the city centre, looking out of the window at the young girls in their minidresses and the lads trailing drunkenly after them. Innocents, really. I wondered what I was getting myself into, knowing that if I went down this road, I couldn't take it back. Although I tried to tell myself that I was just going to have a look, that I was most likely going to turn down Alex's offer as soon as he arrived back in the country, inside me there was a rising fascination with the whole thing. I couldn't ignore the desire my brief encounters with him had sparked, and the gnawing frustration that had driven me into Shane's shop that day hadn't abated. If anything, it was stronger.

'Are you OK?' Kim broke into my reverie.

I nodded, reaching over to turn on the hot air. The PVC leggings, normally sweaty, were doing nothing to help the chill of my nerves.

'I don't know what you're so worried about. Mr Kinky Sex God isn't here, is he, so no one's asking you to do anything. You don't even have to talk to any of these people.'

'But that's the thing. "These people"? Alex is one of them, isn't he? And so might I be, if I carry on seeing him.'

Kim glanced at me sideways.

'I think you're worrying too much, babe. So far, he's just spanked you and given you some nipple clamps. It doesn't mean he's into this whole club scene, or he wants to drag you around in a gimp mask. You need to talk to him.'

I was surprised how blasé she was about the whole thing.

'Well, would you do it?'

She laughed.

'I like my men to do as they're told. Maybe I could do it the other way round, get my Miss Whiplash thing on. I've tied Gary up before; he loved it. Wish I'd gagged him as well – he never shuts up.'

I roared with laughter at her comments, and was feeling a lot more relaxed by the time we pulled into the parking lot for Club Elite. If nothing else, I was sure the night would be an adventure.

From the outside, the place looked more like a hotel, and I felt self-conscious walking up the path to the door in my collar and PVC. When a plump blonde woman in a pink mohair jumper answered the door I thought in horror we had gone to the wrong place, until a girl with pink hair in a leather catsuit, whip in hand, emerged from behind her.

'Er, hi. We phoned earlier. Kelly and Kimberly?'

The blonde woman smiled and extended her hand, which I took awkwardly. Her palms were warm and soft, mine clammy.

'Pleased to meet you. I'm Marilyn. This is Kitty. She'll show you around.'

We went in, and Kitty smiled and motioned us forward.

'If you have any questions,' Marilyn continued, 'I'll be at the reception, or there are waiters in the bar and lounge area who are happy to help. Kitty isn't allowed to talk right now.'

Kitty hung her head. I looked at Kim in bemusement, and could tell she was fighting not to laugh. We followed the silenced Kitty through to the lounge.

'What's the point in her giving us the tour if she can't even speak?' Kim whispered to me – or tried to whisper, I should say, as Marilyn's voice rang through from the hall.

'Kitty needs to learn obedience.'

'Well, that explains everything.'

Kim looked unimpressed. I frowned at her, not wanting to upset our host or our pink-haired guide, but Kitty seemed unconcerned, nodding to us and then towards the bar. Everything looked as it had on the website; in fact, if anything, the place was even more stylish. I was impressed, certainly, though itching to get upstairs and have a look at the playroom. It was still fairly early and I was glad to see there were only a few guests around; a young couple stood smooching at the bar, and a small group of people dressed in various fetish gear sat on the sofas in the chill room. No one looked up or stared as we walked through, and I began to relax; this wasn't too scary.

Five minutes later I stood gawping at the six-foot-high leather cross, as Kim sat down on a huge, round, black cushion with restraints attached.

'This is cool, Kel. It sort of moves with you, look.'

She rolled around on the cushion, which moulded itself to her body. I sat down on it next to her, and had to admit it did feel good, in that childish way that rolling around in a soft-ball pit makes you feel, and it was luxuriously comfortable. The six-foot-high metal cage in the corner of the room, however, was totally freaking me out; that hadn't been visible on the website. The zebra-print swing hung in another corner. Now that did intrigue me, and I had to fight another childish urge to go and jump on it and have a go. I was beginning to understand why they referred to it as a 'play' room.

After a quick look at the bedrooms, which were pretty much as the photos had portrayed, we went back downstairs to the bar and ordered two non-alcoholic cocktails. The barman, topless in black leather trousers, winked at me as he slid the drinks across the bar.

'First time?'

He looked sympathetic. I nodded, looking him up and down. He was gorgeous: dark hair and a ripped body that had been carefully oiled, though without the edginess of Alex. He wouldn't have looked out of place in a boy band. Kim's type more than mine, I thought, and I smiled to myself as she leaned over the bar to talk to him, arms crossed so her cleavage was displayed temptingly. Leaving her to it, I wandered over to the edge of the dance floor, where the couple I had spotted at the bar were now winding against each other, oblivious to anyone else. So far, there had been nothing that had made me regret our visit and want to run screaming for the hills, although Kitty's silencing and the freaky metal cage were pretty bizarre.

As more people started to fill in, including a mixture of pretty boys and girls in fetish wear and the middle-aged, middle-class couples Kim had laughed at, we headed off to the 'chill room'. I had ordered a glass of wine after the not-very-exciting straight cocktail, and I sat back on the sumptuous sofas, crossing my legs and trying to look as if I were a regular.

'Wow. Check her out.'

I looked up in the direction Kim was gawping and saw a tall, red-headed woman in a tiny LBD that just grazed the tops of her lightly muscled thighs. She was older than us, late thirties perhaps, with the type of classic beauty you couldn't help but stare at. Accompanied by a young blond guy, another boy band cut-out, she sauntered over to the empty seats next to us.

'Anyone sitting here?'

I shook my head, feeling suddenly awkward and ungainly as she sat next to me, folding her sleek legs under her with an easy elegance. The blond guy was staring at her with all the adoration of a puppy dog. She smiled at me.

'Have you come for the show?'

'Show?'

'Upstairs.' She jerked her head towards the staircase. 'I'll be whipping Kitty in the playroom. No doubt there'll be something going on in the bedrooms, too.'

I tried not to look as if I was finding the whole conversation completely surreal.

'Are you a regular here, then?'

The redhead chuckled.

'I do this for a living, love. I'm a professional dominatrix. Kevin here,' she patted the knee of the blond, 'is my sub-in-training.'

There it was, that word again. *Submissive*. I needed to know exactly what this entailed. Were there rules? Exactly how submissive was I expected to be? I had never been great at doing what I was told, and I wasn't convinced I was going to be able to start now. Something told me, however, that for Alex that was part of the thrill: if I had been a meek and mild sort of woman I doubted he would find me quite so 'intriguing'.

I looked at the woman for a few moments before deciding to take the plunge.

'I'm really new to this,' I confessed. 'What exactly does it all entail, this sub–dom thing?'

She turned her full attention on me and lifted her knees on to the sofa, settling in more comfortably. I glanced at Kim, not wanting her to feel ignored, to see her flirting with a young black guy in leather trousers. Why were they all in leather trousers, I wondered aimlessly, before turning my attention back to the woman next to me.

'What do you want to know, love?'

She had a low, soothing voice and a way of speaking that immediately put me at ease – not the traditional picture of a Miss Whiplash, but I could see why her eager boy-toy was so enthralled. She was hypnotic.

'I'm thinking of . . . entering a BDSM relationship, but I don't know a lot about it. Hence why I'm here.'

She looked concerned.

'Well, surely you should be asking the other person? Is it . . .?' She nodded towards Kim, and I barked a surprised laugh.

'No! No, it's a guy. My boss, actually. He kind of sprung the idea and then conveniently left the country for a few weeks. So far, there's been a bit of spanking, but that's all. I just feel really naïve about the whole thing.'

She looked thoughtful.

'OK, well, usually a person comes into this lifestyle by being introduced to it by someone else, but it's a bit irresponsible of this guy to proposition you without fully explaining himself.'

I had an inexplicable urge to stick up for Alex.

'Well, he had to go for family reasons, I think, and I'm sure we'll have a full conversation when he gets back. He suggested I do some "research" while he was away. I guess so I could make my own mind up.'

She didn't look convinced. Digging into her purse, she handed the blond a note.

'Go and get me two glasses of wine,' she ordered. That low voice was suddenly sharp, and the blond scuttled away, nodding furiously. I fought the urge not to laugh.

'OK. I'm assuming from what you've said that he wants to top you?'

The blank look on my face prompted her to explain.

'"Top" is the term for the dominant one in the partnership, "bottom" the submissive, or sub, or in some cases slave. Every couple will be different in how far they want to take it. Some people live this lifestyle twenty-four hours a day; for others it's simply a case of being kinkier in the bedroom than the average couple. Others, like my clients, pay for the experience on a regular basis, as an escape from their usual routine. They're usually married,' she added, pursing her lips, as if in disapproval.

'Has he given you any indication how far his tastes run? BDSM could mean anything from the odd spanking to full-on whips, chains, suspension . . .'

She sighed when I looked blank again. Kevin came back with the wine, and I went to thank him, and then thought better of it. Learning already.

The woman rummaged around in her handbag and handed me a stylish business card embossed with a stiletto inside a collar. Above it, her name – Anna Alpha, a name for a comic book superhero, I thought – and a number.

The card was red and black with a vinyl finish. There was no need for any written details of the services she offered – the card said it all.

'I tell you what, give me a ring in the week and we'll go for coffee. You can pick my brains in private, in a more neutral environment.'

'Thank you.'

I slipped the card into my clutch and Anna stood up.

'I need to go and get ready for the floor show. Come up and have a look; the best way to find out if it's for you is to get involved.'

She left, and I nudged Kim, who had moved closer to her latest prey.

'There's something going on upstairs in a bit.'

'Go ahead, hon, I'll be fine down here.'

I rolled my eyes. I'd been intending on her coming with me, but at least she was occupied. I sat, feeling like a third wheel, for the next twenty minutes until Marilyn came into the room and announced upstairs was open. People excitedly followed her upstairs but I crept up nervously, more than a little self-conscious. A skinny guy with long black hair and a huge purple studded collar and leash round his neck winked at me, only to be yanked forward by a muscled guy holding the other end. I shook my head to myself as I headed up the stairs. I couldn't see any of this being Alex's scene. Then again, how well did I really know him?

In the playroom Kitty was strapped naked to the cross, her back to the room. Her pale skin looked flawless and ethereal under the dim lights. She was resting her face on the leather and I could see she was blindfolded, her lips curved in a serene smile, which to me jarred with her situation. Those who had come upstairs crowded into the room and you could feel the atmosphere: a kind of awed, expectant silence. I shifted from one foot to the other, suddenly too hot and uncomfortable in my heels.

Anna swept in. It took me a moment to recognise her as she had tied her long red hair into a ponytail and changed into a PVC all-in-one with a dangerously low cleavage. The shiny black stillettos she wore emphasised her height, and the overall effect was stunning but somewhat intimi-dating. She sashayed over to Kitty with practised ease, sex in every movement, clearly in her element. She grasped a whip in her right hand. I was shocked by how real, how cruel it looked. I realised I'd been expecting a prop, that this whole thing was some kind of elaborate act – but the leather whip was no prop. It looked like the kind of thing you would use to flog a horse. The reality of what I was about to see hit me. Wouldn't it hurt? But the moan Kitty let out when Anna trailed the end of the whip down her back and across her buttocks sounded like need, not pain.

Anna had a look of fierce concentration on her face as she lifted the whip, arm taut, and brought it down across Kitty's back. The girl flinched, and a sigh went around the room. Looking around me I noticed the expressions of desire on the faces that surrounded me; all eyes were on Anna and her willing victim.

It was smotheringly hot in the room now and I tugged at my top, stepping back towards the door. Perhaps look-ing for an easy getaway. With every lash of the whip the tension in the room got more unbearable, and though I didn't find watching Kitty getting 'punished' at all erotic,

I could hardly fail to react to the undercurrent of charged lust. Or the visual tableau. The white curves of Kitty's body against the leather of the cross and the black whip snaking down on her; the shine from the catsuit that hugged Anna's amazing figure against the crimson swing of her hair; all against the backdrop of the dimly lit playroom, with its various devices. It was as though I had wandered into an erotic art house film, all soft focus and shadows. My pulse felt as though it was throbbing between my legs. I tried to imagine being Kitty on that cross, naked and blindfolded, totally at Anna's mercy. The thought of it being me and Alex thrilled me – I couldn't deny that – only without a roomful of voyeurs. And the pain.

Kitty was straining against the leather now, her hands tied together above her head. It was hard for me, a naïve onlooker, to judge whether she was experiencing pleasure or pain. Probably both; she pulled at her bonds as if trying to get away even as she arched her back into the lashes. They were coming harder and faster now, building up to a crescendo, and Kitty's moans were audible in the crowded room. I could see red welts forming on her back and buttocks from the repeated blows; red tiger stripes on her otherwise flawless skin.

Finally it stopped, and another collective sigh went around the room, long and drawn out as if the watchers had been holding their breath simultaneously. I realised with a sudden shock that I had been holding mine; and feeling light-headed and overwhelmed I backed out of the room. As I left I saw Kitty, released from the cross, fall trembling into Anna's arms.

Back in the corridor I slipped into the nearest room,

leaning back into a wall and taking a long breath. A whimpering sound made me look up. I was in the bedroom with the black bed that I had seen earlier, and I wasn't alone. A plump woman with long blonde hair lay spread-eagled on the bed, naked apart from a pair of glossy hold-ups, and it took me a few moments to realise she was tied down at each wrist and ankle. A lithe olive-skinned guy knelt over her, in between her legs, his cock in his hand. I looked away, then back again, transfixed.

'You want it?' he asked her, smiling, and I saw her nod her head furiously.

'Beg,' he demanded of her and she whimpered a please, straining at her bonds.

I felt wrong watching, but at the same time I couldn't look away. The man shuffled up towards her head and lowered his hips, pushing his cock into her open mouth. She sucked at him with hunger, lifting her head off the bed so her long hair fell back on to the sheets, and he bowed his back, pushing further into her mouth.

I was fascinated. I had watched the occasional bit of porn in the past, but I've always found it faintly embarrassing, so this was way out of my comfort level. Yet I didn't seem able to stop staring, and in all honesty I didn't want to. I wanted to see. I moved closer as he pulled away from her mouth to kneel in between her legs again, reaching down to rub her cleft, making her whimper at his touch.

'You're wet,' he remarked in an almost offhand way, and I thought of my date with Alex, when he had made me climax over his knee.

I had to fight the urge to reach down and touch myself.

I watched as he pushed himself inside her, and she bucked her hips against him, unable to move any other way. I had to wonder what that felt like, to be tied up and bound, your body completely in another's hands, unable to do anything but respond. In the dull light I could see the look of sheer abandonment on her face; pure unadulterated desire. She looked intoxicated with it. He gripped her hips and started moving urgently. I was about to take another step closer, hypnotised by the dance of their bodies, when he stopped, and she turned her head and smiled straight at me.

'Do you want to join us?'

Shaken out of my daze, I shook my head furiously, backing off. As I turned to leave I bumped into two of the men I had seen in the playroom, and a couple stood behind them, craning their heads to see into the room. I felt relieved I hadn't been the only one watching, yet also disappointed; the situation went from feeling erotic, if uncomfortable, to plain tacky. I had forgotten where I was. I hadn't stumbled into some forbidden secret; this was most likely a normal night at the club.

Wanting to go, I hurried down the stairs, ignoring two young women who greeted me as I went past, and went back to Kim, who was now chatting to an older man in a suit. I guessed the woman at his side glaring frostily at her was his wife.

'Are you ready?'

She looked up, annoyed, then her expression changed as she saw me. She nodded, knocked her teetotal cocktail back and waved goodbye to the man, who beamed in the direction of her boobs, and his wife, who ignored her. I rushed Kim out of the club, grateful for the shock of the cold air as it hit my skin and raised goosebumps on my arm. Kim looked at me with concern.

'You OK? What went on up there?'

I told her, and she cackled with laughter.

'Oh, wow! I can't believe I missed that! This place is just . . . weird. Fun, but very weird.'

I nodded in agreement as I slipped into the car and rested my head back on the seat. It had indeed been a strange night. Even without the fact that I seemed to have uncovered voyeuristic tendencies I hadn't known I had – although if I'd known of the discoveries to come, perhaps I would have been less concerned.

We drove home in relative silence, my head whirling. I still had Anna's card and planned on phoning her, although, compared to the warm, helpful woman I had met in the lounge, the Anna I had seen up in the playroom had intimidated me. Perhaps that was part of the attraction for those who were happy to get involved in all this: the act of being able to take on an entirely different persona and be somebody else.

I hoped that this didn't mean Alex was putting on an act. The last thing I needed in my life was yet another jerk pretending to be something he wasn't. The thought made me smile. If anything, he had been brutally honest, had – literally – shown his hand.

'You're very quiet,' Kim observed, looking concerned.

'Just wondering what I'm letting myself in for.'

'At least you found out quickly,' she pointed out. 'It's not as if you were dating him for months and all of a sudden he tied you up and whipped out the ball gags.'

I had to laugh. She was right: he had told me what he

wanted, although after the club, I wasn't entirely clear what that was. There seemed to be as many different types of personalities in this lifestyle as there were practices, and I didn't know his preferences. I was pretty sure that if he wanted to tie me down and fuck me in front of a room full of people I would not be impressed. The thought of him tying me down and fucking me, however, had a different effect, which made things tighten low in my belly and the pulse between my legs increase to a steady throb. The image of the girl on the bed came to me: restrained, yet arching up to her lover, desperate for him and not caring that he knew it. Could I be that open, surrender that much?

It was an image that played on my mind as I lay in bed later that night. I ran my hands up my body and over my breasts, picturing Alex's hands and mouth on my skin, wondering how it would feel to be tied down and at his mercy. Helpless and wanting while he fucked me. Even as I slipped my hand between my legs and brought myself to a climax, biting my other hand to stifle my moans, the thought disturbed me as much as it excited me. It wasn't just the thought of whips and chains. It was the sheer need I felt around this man. I had wanted people before, had felt desire, but this was on a different level. I was longing for him to come back, but what – exactly – would that mean for me?

Journal extract

He's back.

He phoned earlier, and he wants to meet tomorrow. I tried not to sound like an overeager schoolgirl but I'm dying to see him. His voice on the phone is so sexy, and he sounded really concerned as well – he actually asked if I wanted to see him, rather than trying to bloody order me. What did he think, that I would have forgotten about him and met someone else in the last few weeks? Perhaps he thought he had scared me off. After all he didn't mention the nipple clamps or the reason for them.

The club scared me, sort of. I don't know that I would want to go to anything like that again. And I think if he had got back earlier in the week I might have had second thoughts about seeing him, but it's been that long now I just want to see him regardless. I'm not going to know if it's what I want or not until I try it, am I, and something tells me he's going to be really good in bed; if his touch that first night is anything to go by . . .

Work has been crap all week. And today I heard Amanda and one of the maths tutors gossiping about how the fit new manager is back from his holidays soon. Bitches. I had to stop myself saying something, I felt like a jealous girlfriend, and then it got me worrying: does he always proposition employees like this? It's not like he wasted much time with me. I don't want to make a fool of myself. I need to stop tying myself up in knots about him.

Ha, just realised what I wrote. Tying myself up in knots . . .

Chapter Seven

His house. He wanted me to go to his house. Alex had phoned me after work that Wednesday night and invited me round for dinner; he was cooking. No mention of anything else, just a normal date.

I tried to tell myself that as I got a cab to his place, but my hands were shaking as I zipped up my purse, a mixture of nerves and excitement. I had picked up the blindfold and butterfly clamps to put into my bag but then thought better of it; I did, however, put on my very best underwear. A lacy black La Perla set with stockings that had cost nearly a month's rent, concealed beneath the same grey dress I had worn the day I met him. The lingerie had been an expensive treat to myself and rarely saw the light of day, so I was hoping the events of the night would justify it. I had pinned my hair up and applied tasteful make-up; perhaps I was deliberately going for a demure look to hide the fact that I was gagging to sleep with him. With the addition of my new glasses I looked more like I was off to a job interview than a date. Hopefully a steamy one.

Alex opened the door and looked me up and down

with appreciation, then grinned at me almost shyly. I was shocked at how good he looked, as if not seeing him for a few weeks had dulled the memory of his visual impact. His wavy brown hair was a touch lighter from the sun, his skin a touch darker, a combination that made his eyes a piercing green. The smell of something good cooking came from over his shoulder, and I grinned back.

'Hey.'

'Hey. How was Cyprus?'

'Amazing. Let me take your coat.'

I stepped into the hall, looking round at his home. He lived on a much nicer side of town than me, and his house was lovely, if very minimalist. Wood floors and white walls greeted me, and from what I could see of the kitchen and lounge they were more of the same. I couldn't help wondering about his bedroom.

He pressed close to me as he took my coat, placing a light kiss behind my ear that made me shudder.

'I like your hair up. These too.' He flicked at my glasses.

'I don't wear them as often as I really should, mostly just for work. I'm quite short-sighted.'

He smiled that wicked half-smile that seemed to tug at his mouth of its own accord.

'I've a good mind to drop in on one of your classes one day, see you in action.'

'Don't you dare.'

I swatted playfully at his arm before following him into the lounge, stomach fizzing with excitement. He was more relaxed than the other times I'd seen him. Maybe because he was in his own home, or was he relieved I'd agreed to see him again instead of running away screaming?

Of course, nearly a month in Cyprus might have had something to do with it. Whichever, he was more at ease, almost playful with me. I liked it. This I could handle.

'What are we eating?'

'Spiced lamb with Mediterranean vegetables,' he said with pride, handing me a small glass of red wine.

'You like to cook?'

Personally, I'm not a huge fan of cooking, certainly not my own, anyway. A man who can cook is always a winner for me.

'I love to. Both my parents are fantastic cooks; they taught me and my sister well.'

'You have a sister? Does she live over here?'

I remembered once again how little I knew about him.

'Yes. She's a teacher, too. You'll like her.'

That made me pause, the idea that he had thought far enough ahead to come to the conclusion that I would like his sister . . . but then maybe he introduced all his dates to her. I squashed the thought before I could make a sarcastic remark and instead sipped my wine demurely, looking at him through my glasses over the rim of my drink. It had the desired effect: he gave a low chuckle and narrowed his eyes at me before turning to the kitchen.

'Just wait there. Dinner will be ready in a minute.'

I relaxed back into the black leather sofa, crossing my legs underneath me. After a moment, he came back in with two plates of exotic-smelling food and laid them on an oak table at the back of the room. I felt at ease, but not enough to stop me saying with jokey suspicion, 'This is all very nice – are you trying to lull me into a false sense of security? Get me all relaxed and well fed and then strap me to a leather cross?'

He raised his eyebrows, surprised. He pulled me out a chair and I went over, regretting my outburst. Still, it needed saying sooner or later and I have never been one for patience. Best to get it out there and dealt with.

'What makes you say "leather cross"?'

Somewhat sheepishly, I told him about Kim's and my visit to Club Elite, as he sat opposite me and seasoned his food. He put the salt down with a bang and looked up at me sharply. I thought he was angry, then saw by the twist of his mouth that he was struggling not to laugh.

'You went where?'

'You suggested I do some "research". I thought I would go and have a look for myself. It was . . . unusual.' To say the least.

'I'm sure. That wasn't really what I had in mind. I thought you might look on Google, read a book, even watch a film.' He laughed again. 'Even I have been known to feel intimidated by those places. I might have extreme tastes, but I think I prefer to keep my sex life in my own home.'

Well, that was a relief. I had been right, then: I had been having trouble seeing Alex wandering around the club in PVC pants, me trailing behind him on a lead. Although his words indicated that he had at least tried the whole club scene.

'So, did you enjoy it?' he asked me. Then he frowned, as a thought occurred to him. 'I assume you didn't get involved with anyone?'

I allowed myself a stab of pleasure at the hint of jealousy

in his voice, before shaking my head firmly. I told him about Kitty, in between mouthfuls of admittedly divine-tasting lamb, but left out the couple in the bedroom. I still wasn't sure how I felt about that, or more to the point didn't yet want to examine how aroused it had made me.

He was quiet for a while after I finished, concentrating on his food. I took a large gulp of wine, waiting for him to speak.

'And how would you feel,' he raised his head and looked straight at me, his eyes intense, 'if that were you on the cross, and me whipping you?'

My thighs tightened.

'I'm not sure. The thought turns me on, it truly does, but I wouldn't want you to hurt me. I take it we would have, like, a safe word?'

He nodded.

'Of course. And in all honesty I should never have spanked you that night without talking about all of this first but you were so very tempting in your innocence. And I know you enjoyed it; I sensed it in you as soon as we met, and I had been itching to get you over my knee ever since you tried to give me the brush-off.'

'But wouldn't you have felt like an idiot if I had jumped up and ordered you out of my house?'

'Absolutely. I probably would have resigned. I didn't exactly think it through; but just so you know, that won't happen again. I won't do anything to you that I'm not sure you want.'

I didn't know myself what I wanted. His certainty was strangely alluring. I didn't voice my thoughts but instead dug back into my meal. I was too nervy to have much of an appetite, a shame considering how good his food was. I hoped he wasn't expecting me to return the favour; I can still to this day only just about whip up a decent pasta bake. Hardly the food of fine dining.

I played with my dinner a little more before laying my cutlery down; he had long since finished and swiftly swooped in to clear the plates. I followed him into the kitchen.

'Can I help?'

'No, no, you're a guest. And I want to show you something. Upstairs.'

I hadn't even had time to digest my dinner, but I followed him up the stairs nevertheless, the oak floors giving way to thick cream carpets. The first door was open, revealing a minimalist bedroom with an array of gadgets neatly stacked under a large plasma TV. Very bachelor pad. The next door was shut, and he hesitated for a moment before opening it.

'This is the spare bedroom. I keep my toys in here.'

I knew what he meant before I even stepped in. This would be his 'playroom'. After the heavy atmosphere of the club, the room I walked into was fairly tame; a bedroom much like the first, except with a smaller version of the cross Kitty had been strapped to in one corner, and pieces of silk at the corners of the headboard that I guessed were meant to be restraints.

Now I knew why he had looked surprised when I had made the quip about leather crosses.

I looked around and then sat on the bed in front of him, giving him my best alluring smile even though my heart was going like a jackhammer.

'Very nice,' I said.

'Don't be flippant. I was worried about showing you this. Although now I know you attend fetish clubs in your spare time, perhaps I shouldn't have been so nervous.'

I laughed.

'It's probably just as well I did. If I had had no idea and then you had brought me back to this, I don't know what I would have thought.'

He came and sat next to me, stroking my knee in small circles. It felt nice.

'Is there anything you want to ask me? I don't want you to feel we have to do anything tonight.'

'I want to do lots of things tonight' – his affection was making me bold – 'but it does bother me: why do you want this? Is it a sadist thing, getting a kick out of hurting people? Because that concerns me.'

'Good God, no.' He looked offended. 'You think I'm some kind of abuser? Come on, now, Kelly, if you really thought that then you wouldn't be here.'

He was right. I was intrigued, not frightened. Scared of where this was going to lead me, perhaps, but not scared of him, not in that way.

'It's hard to explain, but I get off on the idea that you're surrendering to me completely, giving your body to me to do whatever I please, and loving it. That's a beautiful gift. And I'm a man; I suppose there is a bit of the caveman instinct in there. But I would be sickened if I thought you were scared or hurt. This is why I've tried to introduce it slowly.'

'Spanking on a first date and nipple clamps on the second is slowly? I'd love to see your idea of rushing things.'

He had the grace to look embarrassed.

'I've tried to explain about the spanking. And I like you, enough to want to see you regularly, so it must be better I let you know what I'm into before we go any further, surely?'

I thought about that, about stories I'd read about women finding out after years of marriage that their husbands were sneaking off to be stamped on or tied up or whatever. This was infinitely preferable.

He raised his hand to my chin, cupping it and stroking the edge of my face with his thumb. I think he meant it to be affectionate, but it was a strangely erotic gesture. I tipped my head into his hand and nipped his palm. He drew a sharp breath and pulled me into his arms. I went straight for his mouth but he dodged my kiss, nipping my bottom lip and then my cheek, kissing my eyebrows and nuzzling my neck until I was grinding my teeth in frustration.

'Do you want to go into the other room?'

'No.'

And I didn't. All the worries and frustration of the previous weeks had slowly and surely led me to this. I wanted him the way he had been that first night. I wanted him to grab me and order me to come, to put me over his knee like I was his. The desire for it gripped me like velvet ropes. I wasn't going anywhere.

'Here.'

Without meaning to, I looked over at the cross. He followed my gaze, and his hands bunched in my hair.

'There?'

Could I do it? But I already knew the answer.

'Yes.'

He practically dragged me over to the cross, his hands now at my hips, bunching my dress up around my thighs. I was wet already, my breathing shallow. He pushed me into it gently, pulling my arms above my head and fastening them with the restraints. I moaned, pulling on them. They weren't fastened tight enough to hurt, but I certainly couldn't get away. The fact thrilled me rather than scared me, and I arched my back towards him. He made a noise low in his throat and yanked my dress up to my waist, revealing the underwear and stockings.

'Nice.'

His hand trailed over my ass, just brushing across my pussy but not quite touching me. I pushed back against him again only to be rewarded with a sharp slap across my cheeks.

'Wait. You're an impatient little bitch, aren't you?'

Oh, God, yes. I could feel my juices pooling in between my thighs, my face sweaty already against the leather. He pulled my knickers down slowly, too fucking slowly, right down to my shoes. I stepped out of them eagerly, kicking them away, and he used his foot to move my own feet apart before restraining them to the legs of the cross. He stepped back to admire his handiwork.

'My little fuckslut.'

He sounded proud, which should have been at odds with his words. Just as on our first encounter, his dirty talk thrilled rather than offended me, spurring me on to be more wanton, to give him that bit more.

Stepping forward he pressed himself against me,

slipping a hand in between my thighs to my exposed pussy, rubbing his fingers insistently against my clit.

'I'm going to whip you, slut.'

'Yes, Sir.'

Every feminist instinct I had screamed at me to tell him to fuck off, to react as I normally would if such words were aimed at me in any other situation, but a deeper need overrode any such concerns. The way I felt, he could call me anything he damn well wanted.

'Oh, God,' he panted.

His breath was as ragged as mine. So much for control.

'We need a safe word before we do this.'

I had forgotten about the safe word, and right then was in no fit state to think of anything sensible. Believe me, I have looked back at this moment and cringed many times since.

'Something neutral that has nothing to do with anything we may be doing.'

I blurted out the first thing that came to my mind.

'Potato?'

'What? OK, fine. Potato it is.'

I could hear the laughter in his voice and cursed myself for lightening the mood. I had liked it just fine how it was. But perhaps it wasn't such a bad idea; I couldn't think of a better way to neutralise a too-kinky or overly intense situation than by randomly shouting out 'potato'. For the record, I don't even like potatoes.

Behind me he moved away. I thought for an awful, heart-stopping minute that I had brought us too far back to reality and he was going to stop, but with relief I heard him opening and shutting a drawer. As he approached

I could see the whip in his hands. He held it up. It was smaller and with strips of fabric, not the cruel horsewhip Anna had used.

'It's a flogger,' he told me. 'Better for beginners.'

He set it down and then reached for my head, removing the glasses and fastening a blindfold over my eyes. I wasn't too sure about that.

'I can't see what you're doing.'

'That's the point. It heightens the sensation, and ups the element of surprise. Now shut up.'

I shut up.

He stepped back, and I had an acute feeling of aloneness, unable to feel where he was while I was strapped and exposed like so much quivering flesh. I went to speak but then felt movement close behind me.

The first lash shocked me. It was lighter than the spanking, yet stung a hell of a lot more.

'Push your ass out to me.'

I did it, even as I felt myself flinch as I sensed his arm move. He brought the flogger down again, harder this time, and then again, and again. I cried out, protesting at the stinging pain, but it wasn't a no, it wasn't the safe word. As much as my ass was killing me, my pussy and nipples throbbed with a very different feeling. If there is a fine line between pleasure and pain, as they say, then Alex had certainly discovered mine. I was desperate for him to touch me.

'Do you want more?'

'Yes, Sir.'

'More what? What do you want? Tell me, baby. Beg for it.'

I could feel wetness trickling down my leg. My wetness. I wanted to cross my legs to hide it but couldn't, they were forced apart by the restraints. There was no way of hiding how turned on I was, but that was what he wanted. My complete exposure to him.

'Whip me. I want you to whip me, Sir. Please. Hard.'

Where that last word came from I don't know, but he responded in kind, delivering a cruel blow that made me scream. A little too hard, but I was reluctant to safe word and stop the whole thing.

He must have sensed it, though, because he rubbed his hands soothingly over my exposed buttocks, kneading softly, then moved his hand to my pussy again, slipping two fingers inside me. I was soaking. He added another finger.

'Soon I'll be able to get my whole hand inside you. You fucking dirty little bitch. I'm going to make you come on my hand, then force my cock down your throat until you gag on it. And you will love it. Won't you?'

I moaned out a barely coherent yes, inexplicably turned on by his words, filthy words which right then sounded like erotic endearments, and he gave my hair a sharp pull from the nape of my neck before stepping away. I braced myself for another blow.

'Relax, baby. It will hurt less.'

I tried to obey, but instinct made me tense up as I felt rather than heard the flogger coming towards me. The blow was a lot less brutal than the last, thank God, and I started to enjoy the pain, if such a thing is possible. After every few blows he stopped and rubbed me with his hands, soothing some of the stinging. The combination of the harsh punishment and the intermittent affection spun my senses. Every nerve felt raw, every sensation heightened. Time seemed to stretch and follow unknown rules of its own. I felt almost weightless, soaring, and hardly aware of the pain that was no longer pain but pure sensation.

'You like it, don't you, baby? My little bitch. Scream for me.'

'Oh, fuck, yes.'

'Louder.'

'Yes. Yes, I like it.'

He delivered one last, stinging blow that made me yelp, and then stopped abruptly. His breath was coming in loud gasps from his exertions, and I heard him pulling off his top. He pressed his upper body against me and he was as sweaty as I was. He nibbled roughly at my neck.

'Good girl,' he breathed into my ear. 'Good girl. I think you deserve some relief.'

'Please, Sir,' I moaned.

My body throbbed with need; my pussy was liquid fire, I was so desperate to come. I arched my back, waiting for his hand, but felt instead a blunt object. I tensed, wondering what in the hell he was doing before realising it was the other end of the flogger. He slid it into me with ease, for I was so turned on there was no resistance, and then out again until it was slick with my juices. He rubbed it against the swollen nub of my clit and then dipped it again inside me. I groaned.

'Please make me come,' I begged, with no need for prompting from him, no hesitation now in my pleas.

'I'm not going to touch you. You're going to come on the handle for me.'

He eased the flogger back out of me and pressed it against that throbbing spot again, this time leaving it resting there without moving his hand.

'Make yourself come.'

'Alex, no, please.'

He pressed the handle more firmly against my tender and swollen pussy, but didn't move it.

'If you want to come, then do it yourself, girl. Make yourself come for me.'

I hesitated, torn between outrage and humiliation and a desperate need to release the tension in my body. I couldn't even stand up straight; I was hanging on the wrist restraints, my arms quivering from being held up above my head.

'Do it.'

He sounded as needy as me, and that was enough. I rocked my hips against the whip handle and he increased the pressure, at the same time reaching his other hand up to grab my hair and pull my head back. I rocked my hips faster in an almost frenzied rhythm, and he whispered into my ear. He was softer now, less demanding, as my body took over and did as I had been bidden.

'Go on, baby, do it. Make yourself come for me.'

I gave one last desperate rock that tipped me over the edge and I screamed into the leather as I climaxed. It was the most intense orgasm I had ever had, and seemed to go on and on, the contractions coming from deep in my belly. I shuddered to a finish, a sob coming from my throat, and sagged against the cross. He kissed my neck and back with tenderness, then untied the restraints. I went to pull down my dress, but he stopped me.

'We haven't finished yet. Take it off. I want you naked.'

My hands fumbling to obey, I pulled my dress over my head and took off my bra with clumsy fingers, leaving me in just my stockings and shoes. He unzipped his trousers, and my insides twisted. Finally, were we going to have sex?

Unfortunately not.

'Kneel down and open your mouth.'

I obeyed, opening my mouth for him and watching eagerly as he pushed his bottoms down over his hips. His cock was thick, thick enough that I knew it would be a stretch to fit him in my mouth, but I wanted to do it, wanted to please him as he had me.

But he wouldn't even allow me that much. He stepped towards me, but stopped just short of his cock touching my mouth. He rubbed himself lazily and without any hint of embarrassment, his movements controlled. I reached for him only for him to slap my hand away.

'Put your hands behind your back.'

I did as I was told, even though I was by then burning with frustration. He rubbed himself faster, his eyes dark as he approached his own climax. I licked my lips, my mouth dry from being open.

'Open your mouth. Wider.'

He sounded close, his voice breaking, so I tipped my head back and offered my mouth to him. He growled as he came and grabbed the back of my neck, finally pushing his twitching cock into my mouth as he climaxed in thick, salty streams down my throat that went on and on until I gagged. He withdrew, panting, and I swallowed heavily and ran my hands through my hair.

'Can I get up now?'

He nodded, zipping himself back up. I thought for a desperate minute he would be as abrupt as that first time – order me to leave, even – but as he came over to me his face was soft. He kissed me on the lips with a smile, his mouth curving against mine.

'That was amazing. You were amazing.'

'But we didn't have sex.' I pointed out the obvious.

'Not yet. I want you desperate for me before I fuck you.'

I was pretty sure I was there already, but wasn't about to argue with him. In all honesty I was tired, achy and hungry again. Still, I pulled a face. He tutted.

'Good things come—'

'To those who wait? Yeah, I get it.'

'I was going to say: to those who do as they are told.'

I resisted the urge to stick my tongue out at him. Not a good look.

'I'll put the shower on for you. Or maybe a hot bath will be better; you'll be tired.'

As usual it was more an order than a suggestion but I shook my head firmly.

'I want to go home. I have four classes tomorrow and besides, I need time to digest all this.' I waved my hand at the room.

He kissed me again, but not so quickly that I missed the disappointment in his eyes. Would he have asked me to stay? But the moment was gone.

'I understand, but please, look after yourself when you get in, and call me if you need anything. Playing like this can take it out of you. Can I see you soon, maybe lunch this week? Just lunch.'

The smile I gave him was tired, but genuine. Just lunch sounded great. As he called me a cab I wondered if I would give him the wrong idea, leaving like this; it wasn't like me not to want at least some cuddle time after sex, but I had meant what I said. I did need time to digest everything.

For even though we hadn't fucked, I felt the same sense of a line having been drawn as I had when I lost my virginity; there was no going back now. Even if I never saw Alex again, I knew I wouldn't be the same person, at least sexually, as I had been before I stepped into that bedroom.

What bothered me now was: just how far would I be prepared to go?

Journal extract

This is getting crazier and crazier. I really like Alex, not just fancy him; there's something about him when he's not pulling the 'Mr Dominant' act that I'm really warming to. I want to carry on seeing him.

But the sex stuff worries me. Since when have I been the kind of girl who likes being strapped to crosses and whipped?

It was so good, though, so intense. I can't help wanting to go further with him. I just feel so naïve about it all. And worried where it will end up.

I phoned Anna from the club to ask if we could talk. I barely know her, but who else can I ask? She invited me round tomorrow; turns out she doesn't live far away. Do I really want to talk about all of this with a stranger? She was lovely on the phone, really chatty, and a neutral ear might be best. Maybe she can answer my questions.

I have so many.

Chapter Eight

The next evening after work I found myself sitting in Anna's kitchen, nursing a cup of tea. The cosy kitchen, with its wooden table and chairs and checked tablecloth, was a stark contrast to the setting in which I had last seen her, and with her fabulous body hidden in ripped jeans and a polo neck and hair up in a bun, Anna herself looked nothing like the hard-faced dominatrix that had so ruthlessly whipped Kitty. Although I was to learn never to judge a book by its cover, right now I was bemused by the change in her appearance. She had struck me as the kind of woman who probably wore her heels to bed.

Anna was patient as I stammered through an account of my date with Alex. It felt strange to be telling her something so intimate, but I was desperate to talk to someone who wouldn't think I was weird, or make flip comments, like Kim.

I had woken up to an affectionate phone call from Alex and the offer of lunch tomorrow. As much as I had been thrilled to hear from him, I had been coy, my face as red as my ass cheeks, as his voice evoked memories of last night.

I had woken up with a dull throbbing on my bottom that had turned to a sting as I got up. Twisting round in the mirror, I'd been shocked to see vivid red and purple marks across my butt. How could I go for lunch with a man who had marked me like this? After I had asked him to.

I tried to explain myself to Anna, waving my hands as I spoke.

'I just don't see how I can enter a relationship with him, and carry on in the bedroom this way. The two just don't seem compatible.'

'I think that's your issue,' she said gently. 'You're seeing the fact that he wants your sexual relationship to include BDSM as something seedy. Or perhaps you're worried about things getting too intense? The best dom–sub relationships, I think, actually occur when the two people are in love or at least care about each other as individuals, but it does stir up some intense emotions. As well as causing you to be less careful with practical matters than you should be.'

I frowned. Was she lecturing me on contraception? She hurried to explain herself.

'If you're engaging in some of the more extreme practices, you have to know what you're doing and how to use the equipment. Couples who are more engrossed in each other than the practice itself can actually be less conscientious about such things. It's a fine line.'

I studied Anna. She seemed very detached from the whole subject, discussing it as if she were a therapist rather than a professional dominatrix. Maybe she was right; without a full relationship to accompany the sex, wouldn't it be just a series of empty encounters, much like I imagined

Anna must experience with her clients? We had talked a little about her job and some of her clients' more bizarre needs, and I was praying Alex's tastes wouldn't run too far to the exotic.

I shook my head as Anna offered me a cigarette; I have, thankfully, never smoked.

'You need to establish with him what he means when he talks about a "submissive" and what you are and are not happy to do. Establish your "hard limits", boundaries you absolutely will not cross. Of course, some limits you will only find by testing them.'

I nodded in agreement with her. I had already lain awake all night questioning my enjoyment of having been whipped. I've always been a bit of a baby where pain is concerned, so my reaction to the flogging had shocked me; he had taken me to a point where I had almost wanted him to hurt me and to hit me harder, and then to a point where it hadn't hurt at all.

'The thing is, it was a different kind of pain, if that makes sense.'

'Endorphin rush. The pain coupled with sexual desire; it's a potent cocktail. The moment of surrender is an amazing feeling.'

I remembered the intense orgasmic rush when I had given in and rocked myself to a climax on the handle of the flogger. I took a big gulp of my drink to avoid meeting Anna's piercing gaze. In all honesty, I was embarrassed at my eagerness to give myself over to Alex, so much so that the prospect of lunch with him the next day had me again fizzing with nerves. I was at least determined to be more knowledgeable before I saw him again, hence the visit to Anna. Plus the fact that she intrigued me in her own right. There was a husky-voiced earthy glamour to her that reminded me of a forties silver-screen star; maybe I was hoping some of it would rub off on me.

'It's sometimes referred to as "subspace", the almost soaring, out-of-body feeling a submissive can experience through the combination of pleasure and pain and the endorphin rush. It's addictive, and intense. Of course, not everyone experiences it.'

'I think I have.'

I told her about the way I had felt on Alex's cross, the way time had disappeared and blurred, and then how afterwards I had felt achy and irritated, wanting to be alone. But then I had missed him desperately as soon as I was.

'That's the drop you get after flying in subspace; it's like a crash, a withdrawal. It's perfectly normal after such an intense physical experience.'

She was so matter-of-fact. I realised I didn't want my experience with Alex picked apart and dissected like this, given everyday labels as though it was a common experience. Although, in Anna's world, it no doubt was.

'The perfect sub is pliant and obedient,' Anna went on, 'and always eager to please. This may be just in the bedroom, but there are a lot of people who live that lifestyle every moment they are with their master or mistress – to the point of being told what to wear, eat, the lot. More of a true slave than a sub.'

I screwed my face up at that.

'Why would you want to give anyone that much power over you?'

I didn't get it.

'It takes responsibility for your own choices away for at least a while; it can be a liberating feeling. So I'm told, anyway. I'm most definitely a dominant. Some people "switch" between roles and are happy to take turns being top or bottom.'

I certainly couldn't imagine Anna at the other end of a whip.

'But then, what do you get out of it?'

I was beginning to understand the appeal of submitting, but couldn't see why anyone would want to be a dominant for any reason other than the sadistic. But then Alex had said how much of a turn-on it was for him; not the fact I was in pain but the offering of myself into his hands. Either way, it sounded suspiciously like a power trip. I wondered what Alex's reaction would be if I asked him if we could try things the other way round.

'You need to ask him that.' Anna effectively dodged answering the question for herself. 'It can create strong emotional ties, this kind of relationship, especially if it's your first time. A lot of doms relish the adoration they get from their sub, as well as the feeling that they are theirs not just to pleasure but to protect.'

I grinned at that. I had to admit to loving how attentive and alpha-male Alex seemed towards me. I was turning into a fluttery romance-novel heroine.

'I'd like to know more about the different kinds of practices,' I said.

When I had initially looked on the web with Kim, there had been some bizarre results to our searches. Whipping was one thing, but electric shocks and being hung from the ceiling? Perhaps not so much fun.

'People's tastes within BDSM are as varied as anyone's sex life,' Anna yawned and stretched in her chair like a cat. 'At the mild end there's "sensation play", which involves ice cubes, fur etcetera, usually while tied up, and at the very extreme end what we call "edge play". Well, you've got knife play, auto-erotic asphyxiation . . .'

'That's supposed to be what killed Michael Hutchence,' I shuddered, recalling reading about the singer's death while eating my cornflakes before school, before the paper was swiftly snatched away by my stepdad.

'All the more reason why you should only be carrying out practices like that with someone you trust or a professional, preferably both. Some people who are heavily into the club scene will actually undergo "training", whether in submission or domination. Some practices really do require expert knowledge.'

'Well, I'm certainly not into anything like that. What about "collaring"? It was mentioned on a few of the sites we found.'

'A collar is literally that: a collar round your neck, although some subs wear variations on their wrists or ankles. It's a sign of commitment to your dom, an indication to others that you're taken.'

'Like a wedding ring,' I laughed, and Anna chuckled with me.

'Exactly. They're a physical contract, if you wish. There are traditionally three types, like stages of commitment. It's all quite formal. I've heard of people actually having written contracts drawn up. But all of this is more for people who are dedicated to the lifestyle, regardless of whether they're in a relationship or not.'

'I don't understand.'

'Well, say you were to decide you were a submissive, not just for this Alex but in general. So if you weren't with him you would be looking for a new dom, or heavily on the club scene subbing for different people. There are a lot of online communities where people meet as well. This Alex could be a guy who wants a normal standard relationship, but just likes a bit of S and M in the bedroom. The fact he's got a playroom in his home indicates some level of dedication, though.'

'He certainly seems to know what he's doing,' I admitted. 'I think it's a definite need for him.'

My stomach twisted at the thought of Alex having legions of 'subs' in and out of his playroom. Anna frowned at me.

'You're not just going along with this to please some guy?'

I laughed.

'No! I am enjoying it, so far. I've surprised myself.'

She smiled at me, her eyes kind.

'Then just go with it. You know where I am if you've got any questions. Do you want another drink?'

I nodded. I had nothing to rush home for except a stack of lesson plans and marking. I watched her move around the kitchen gracefully. She had that same air of self-assurance that Alex exuded; well, they were cut from the same cloth in a way, I supposed.

'Do you ever switch?' I asked.

She looked surprised.

'No. I have tried, with an ex who was happy to switch roles, but to be honest I just wasn't very good at it. I could never let go, and if you can't surrender to some degree then the pain is just that: painful. I used to safe word after just a few spanks,' she laughed, then went on: 'But I'm glad I had the experience. There's a saying within the BDSM community that you are a better top from having been a bottom, and I know a lot of doms who used to be submissives, and a few vice versa, too.'

I pictured myself brandishing a whip, not sure if I liked the image or not, though I imagined the power would be a kick.

'And now you do this for a living. Does it make a difference? Doing it professionally, I mean.'

Anna looked down at her cup for a few moments and I regretted being so personal, but then she looked up at me and nodded.

'It's harder than you would think. Like I said, the sub–dom relationship by its nature can create quite an intense bond, but of course I have to remain very detached with clients. I've had a couple become almost obsessed, and had to stop seeing them. Retaining a professional boundary is so important, but of course pushing boundaries is what BDSM is all about.'

Or finding them, I thought. Anna pushed two books over the table towards me.

'Have a read of these.'

I looked at the covers: *The Story of O* and *Exit to Eden*. I hadn't heard of either of them, although I recognised one of the authors; I had her more popular horror fiction on my bookshelves.

'Thanks,' I said, reading the blurbs. Light bedtime reading they were not.

We chatted for a little while longer, about TV programmes and shoes, until I said I had to get on. Anna walked me to the door, kissing my cheek as she said goodbye, before leaving me with a parting shot I would mull over later that night.

'Remember: it sounds contradictory, but ultimately the submissive is the one that calls the shots.'

'How's that?'

'Because the dominant is bound to respect your boundaries, and to stop on your say-so. So the dominant can never truly let go, at least not without the permission of the sub. It's quite a power.'

Her words stayed with me all day. Maybe I had more control over this than I thought. One question remained, though: how I would use my new-found power?

Walk away from what he was offering – or embrace it?

Journal extract

Really interesting talk with Anna. I'm so glad I went to see her. She helped clarify a few things for me in terms of how it all works, but regarding me and Alex . . . I'm not sure if I'm now just even more confused.

It's exciting, in a way, not knowing what might happen, and all these new feelings – but I feel a bit lost. Like I don't really know where this is heading.

I suppose the obvious answer is to talk to Alex. It's ridiculous that I feel shy around him after the things we've done.

I feel like I should tell him I spoke to Anna.

Lunch tomorrow! In spite of everything . . . I can't wait.

Chapter Nine

Alex looked at me as if I had gone out of my mind.

'You went to talk to a professional dominatrix? My God, woman, you don't do things by halves, do you?'

I giggled, leaning back in my chair. As I moved, I felt the sting on my buttocks against the bruises. They were still so sensitive. The twinge of pain, however, brought with it a rush of desire each time, and I looked at his full lips, imagining his mouth on my body. Three days of not seeing him had left me hungry for more.

He had picked me up for lunch outside work, and I had waved at Margaret out of the window, enjoying her surprised glare. Alex had laughed, squeezing my knee and leaving his hand there. We were less awkward with each other than we had been; it was as if some barrier had been crossed, some door opened. I felt young and happy next to him, and delighted when he pulled up outside Pierre's, a fancy French eatery I had never been able to afford to eat in. We sat at a table outside, basking in the warm spring sun.

'I needed someone neutral to talk to. Who knew what she was on about.'

Alex rubbed his hand over his chin. He hadn't shaved, and the dark stubble made him look less clean-cut and even more tempting.

'I can see why you would have gone to her. But in future, can we at least agree that you'll discuss these things with me?'

He looked concerned, and I wondered if I had hurt his feelings by talking to someone else. Or maybe he was worried about exposure?

'You're not bothered that Margaret saw us?'

'It will give her something to gossip about, won't it? But I hope you won't be discussing our relationship at work?'

I smiled.

'We're having a relationship now?'

Alex narrowed his eyes at me, asking me out of the blue, 'Are you dating anyone else?'

'No. I mean, I was kind of seeing someone, but not now.'

'Who?'

He sounded jealous. I told him, very briefly, about Shane, although I left out the last time we had had sex, on the couch in his shop. Alex speared his food as if stabbing it. He was definitely jealous.

'I don't want you seeing him any more.'

'He's my friend,' I said softly. 'I see him all the time. But I'm not sleeping with him any more. I told him about you.'

He nodded, looking pacified.

'And you? You're not involved with anyone?'

'No.' He looked annoyed I had even asked; a bit rich, I thought, given it had been his choice of conversation. 'I prefer to date exclusively.'

'So we're officially dating, then?' I grinned, loving his use of words that sounded to me old-fashioned. I hardly ever heard my friends use 'dating' any more; it was always 'seeing' or something equally casual.

'I'm not entirely sure what we're doing. But there are plenty of things I would like to do to you.'

His eyes said sex and other, darker things. I felt bold, for once. Ready to play his games. I glanced around to make sure no one was within listening distance before sliding a foot up the leg of his trousers.

'Anything I can help you with . . . Sir?'

He stared at me for a second in surprise, before smirking and nodding towards my plate.

'Finish your food. I need to get you back.'

I felt deflated, removed my foot from his leg and turned my attention back to my plate. He didn't speak, just sat there watching me eat, until I put my fork down, blushing under his scrutiny.

'Go to the toilet while I pay,' he ordered quietly, 'and take your knickers off.'

I stared at him, eyes wide, but unable to deny the melting feeling in the pit of my belly, my insides flipping as he looked at me steadily. So he did want to play.

I made my way inside to the toilets, which were clinically pristine, feeling a delicious sense of naughtiness as I passed two women deep in conversation by the basins. I slipped into a cubicle and locked the door, then leaned back against the door for a minute before carefully sliding my knickers off and popping them into my handbag. I was wearing a V-neck and a pencil skirt, perfect sedate-teacher wear that now felt revealing, knowing I was bare beneath.

I waited to hear the two women leave, but they didn't seem to be going anywhere anytime soon, so I flushed the toilet to make a show of having actually used it and stopped in front of the mirrors to fluff out my hair and apply some lip gloss. I was surprised at how much difference a lack of underwear made; I felt almost unbearably naked, acutely aware of the air against my most intimate parts as I left the toilets and made my way back to Alex, who was paying the bill at the counter. He offered me his arm.

'Ready?' he said, eyes twinkling with our shared knowledge of my naked state.

I nodded and he steered me out of the restaurant, holding open the door for me while thanking the waiter, who smiled cheerily at me. I hurried out before my blushes became noticeable, unable to meet the poor guy's eyes. Alex held the car door open, his composure still perfectly cool, still in control, in contrast to my flustered state. I was getting wet under my skirt, could feel it on my thighs, and as I slid into the car I was careful to keep my legs together. Getting in and out of a car in a pencil skirt is never the easiest of tasks, let alone when knickerless and being ordered around by a very sexy control freak.

I sat in silence as Alex drove, looking over at him in surprise when he went in the opposite direction from work, taking me instead down the quieter roads that led to the local park.

'Lift your skirt, let me see you,' he growled.

I obeyed, inching it up bit by bit until it was around my waist, feeling ridiculously exposed and having to resist the compulsion to cover myself with my hands. I was wet, my clit responding to the fresh air against me. It was such a wrong thing to be doing, so out of place, and the knowledge of that turned me on even more. Alex glanced over, taking his eyes off the road briefly to take in the sight of my body. Although he kept his gaze dispassionate, I saw that his hands were gripping the steering wheel so tightly that his knuckles were white.

'Open your legs,' he demanded. I sucked in my breath sharply, but did as I was told. I was desperate for him to touch me. He turned off the road into a layby and I looked around frantically. He couldn't be planning on doing anything here, surely? It was a quiet road but even so, visions of being caught and led away in cuffs danced before my eyes.

Alex switched off the engine and turned to me, drinking in the sight of me sitting there naked from the waist down, my legs slightly parted, waiting for him. My inner thighs trembled.

'Beautiful,' he murmured, bending his head to kiss me. I responded to him eagerly, spontaneous whimpers coming from my throat as he invaded my mouth with his tongue. Shamelessly I pushed my hips towards him but he pulled back, smiling.

'Undo your blouse,' he said, his voice low with lust.

Frustrated and shaking with anticipation, I fumbled at my blouse, revealing my breasts in a perfunctory black bra. Alex reached for them, lifting the cups of my bra so my breasts were released into his hands. He cupped them carefully, feeling their weight, moulding his hands to their curves and brushing the pads of his thumbs over each nipple. My breath was ragged. He pushed them together and then bent his head, giving a long, languorous lick that took in both nipples, then blew on them lightly, making me squirm in his hands. He held my breasts so that my nipples were together and then slowly, tantalisingly, put them both in his mouth, drawing his teeth over them and then sucking down on them. Hard. The sensation went through me like an electric shock, straight from my nipples down to my now-insistently-pulsing clit. I gasped, arching my back, and he continued sucking on them harder, until I could hardly bear the intensity of it. He finally drew back, and then rolled one nipple between his fingers before suddenly pinching and twisting it, with a cruel enough pressure that I yelped. Yet as soon as the momentary pain had gone, a flood of desire followed it. My hands trembled as I reached for him, but he pushed them away.

'You won't be able to safe word, so if you want me to stop, tap my thigh twice.'

I frowned, not understanding. Why couldn't I safe word?

'You can't speak with your mouth full, Kelly,' he said, as if explaining something patiently to a small child.

I must have been crimson, as I felt my face burning instantly. He sat back in his seat and motioned towards his trousers.

'On your hands and knees. Take me in your mouth.'

I scrambled to get into position in the cramped confines of his car, finally managing to get on all fours on the seat and lean over his lap. I struggled with his zipper, my fingers all turning to thumbs. His cock sprang free, proud and erect, and I felt the heat of him against my face. I saw his hand move at the other side of him and heard a soft whirring, and as the air hit my naked ass I realised he had wound down the window.

'Look at you, showing yourself off like that,' he murmured.

It was a clever twist; although there was no one around to see me, the sting of the cool air against my skin brought home to me with stark reality exactly where I was and what I was about to do, with my bits bobbing unashamedly in the air as I bent over him.

He pushed his cock into my mouth without ceremony, sliding himself in as far as he could before he hit the back of my throat. I swallowed around his cock and heard him moan under his breath, then began to move my mouth up and down on him, sucking on his shaft and swirling my tongue around the swollen head. But this was to be on his terms, not mine, and his hands came down to hold my head still as he thrust himself in and out of my mouth. I tried to angle myself to get a better position to take him deeper, but his hands held my head in place as he moved and his cock hit the back of my throat. I retched and he paused, as if waiting to see if I would 'tap out', but I kept my hands where they were. I wanted him. I was quivering with need, and pushed my thighs together to ease the ache in my pussy. There were goose pimples on my flesh from the cold air.

He resumed his rhythm, his movements faster, and I tried to relax my throat, allowing him to thrust in and out of my mouth. I kept my lips tight around him and applied as much suction as I could in such a compromised position. I loved the feel of him in my mouth and was aroused in spite of my discomfort. He growled low in his throat, his hands bunching in my hair, pushing himself further up into my mouth. My jaw ached and my eyes were watering, but I felt a huge sense of satisfaction as he came with a loud cry, pumping into my mouth in thick streams. I swallowed, and then again and again as it kept on coming, before he finally released my head and collapsed back in his seat with a groan. I wiped my mouth, tasting him on my lips.

'That was fantastic. You are one very sexy bitch, Miss Lawrence.'

His voice was deep and lazy, post-orgasmic. Unlike mine, for I was still strung up like a bow, craving his touch. I struggled to sit up and adjust my clothing, looking at him to see what he would do next, but he was winding up the window and starting the car. He smiled at my shocked – and no doubt somewhat indignant – expression, before leaning over and kissing my lips with a gentleness that seemed out of place, given the situation.

'I told you, I want you desperate for me before I fuck you. I want you to beg for it.'

I was damn near prepared to, and to hell with any passers-by, but he was pulling away and turning the key. I shrugged my coat on, trying to ignore my aching nipples as the material brushed over them. I reached in my handbag for my knickers, but he touched my wrist, stopping me.

'Leave them off. I want you to feel how wet you are for me at work this afternoon. So I know you're thinking about me.'

As we pulled up at the college he looked relaxed as he leaned over to kiss my cheek. All right for some, I thought, resentful. I wasn't sure how much more of this frustration game I could take.

'Do you have plans for the weekend?'

'I'm meeting a few friends for a drink on Friday,' I said, wondering if I should invite him, but then thinking better of it.

We were still getting to know each other, after all, and I wasn't sure how Shane would feel, not to mention the fact that Kim knew way too much and I would be worried about her blurting something out.

'I'm free Saturday. Are you asking me out?'

He chuckled at my tone. It was probably a little pointless, I admit, attempting to be aloof after my antics just a few moments earlier. I had never been so subservient giving head. It was something I had always associated with feeling in control, or at least with being the one doing the giving. This had been something else entirely; he had taken his pleasure from me ruthlessly.

'I am, yes. I'd like to actually take you out and do something, away from the kinky stuff, shall we say. Get to know you in other ways.'

I smiled shyly, feeling pleased and somehow flattered.

'That would be nice.'

I had to hurry to class then, only just making it, the room already half full of students. As I began to gabble on about grammar my head was on anything but, and I was painfully aware of my wet, naked pussy underneath my skirt. I could hardly believe what I had just done. Alex was bringing out a side to me I hadn't even been aware of. I resolved to escape to the toilet at the first chance I got, so I could put my underwear back on. It was an hour and a half, in between classes, before I had a moment to myself. I dashed to the toilet, only to hear my phone beeping in my handbag. Alex.

Are you on a break? I can't stop thinking about you.

My heart leapt. Nice to know I wasn't the only one. I texted back in a rush.

Briefly. In loo, putting pants back on.

Don't you dare. I want you to make yourself come for me.

What? I stared at the message, wondering what to reply, when the phone rang, his name flashing on the screen.

'Hello?'

'I want to hear you come. You must be desperate to by now.'

I hesitated. I had never done anything like this before and felt intensely vulnerable, even more so than I had in his playroom when he had ordered me to make myself come on the handle.

'Where are you?'

'In my office, I've only got a minute. Do it. You don't have to talk, just let me hear you.'

I put my bag down and leaned back against the wall, phone at my ear. Feeling foolish, I lifted my skirt and gave a contrived moan into the handset. Being put on the spot had never been my forte and the idea of phone sex normally had me cringing with embarrassment. But as soon as I touched myself my moans became real enough. I was still wet from the car, and my clit responded to my touch greedily, beginning to stiffen under my fingertips. I rubbed myself deftly, remembering his mouth on my breasts, his cock in my mouth, and the way he had exposed me in the car. I was barely aware of my soft moans into the phone as my touch grew more frantic, seeking the release he had denied me earlier.

'Are you close?'

He sounded as if he was gritting his teeth. The thought of him sitting in his office getting turned on as he listened to me, stroking himself even, was enough to tip me over the edge.

'Yes. Alex . . .' I let out his name in a long breath as I climaxed, my pussy clenching around my fingers, hips bucking against the wall. I lay back against the cold plaster as the waves subsided, my breath coming in gasps into the speaker.

'Good girl. I must go. I'll phone you later.'

And the phone cut out abruptly.

Flustered and weak after my orgasm, I tidied myself up and ran off to my next class, with Alex – as he seemed to be more and more these days – still firmly at the forefront of my mind.

Chapter Ten

True to his word, when Alex took me out that Saturday night, it was very much a 'proper' date. We went to the pictures to watch an Adam Sandler film, giggled like schoolkids and threw popcorn at each other. I started it, naturally, and was pleasantly surprised when he responded with a shocked laugh rather than the stern stare I was becoming accustomed to. I was still giggling as we walked to my front door.

As I put the key in the lock I felt his hand on the small of my back moving down to cup my ass and I turned to him, pressing my body against his.

'I've had such a lovely night.'

I leaned up to kiss him and nibbled on his lower lip.

'As have I. It's been a while since I've been to the cinema. And certainly not in such good company.'

'Ooh, you charmer,' I teased, winding my arms around his neck and standing on my tiptoes – I was wearing flats – before pressing my mouth to his.

He kissed me back, opening my mouth wider with his and claiming it with his tongue, in a way that made me think of other things. Instantly I was aroused, pushing my lower body against his as I felt the slow burn of lust. I wanted him, and when both of his hands grabbed my ass and his kiss grew more urgent, I moaned involuntarily into his mouth. We broke away from each other as I heard steps and a couple walked past the porch. I giggled, like a teenager caught snogging by her parents. Alex's eyes were heavy-lidded with desire.

'Are you coming in?'

I pushed the door open. I was expecting a 'yes', and I felt my face drop as he shook his head.

'I mustn't tonight. I've got a really early start, and if I stay I wouldn't be getting a lot of sleep. So, as much as I would love to, I can't.'

He sounded perfectly composed, even after a kiss that had left me weak at the knees.

I tried to regain my composure, nodding.

'That's fine' – was it hell – 'I've got a ton of marking to do.'

He kissed me on the forehead and went back to his car. I watched him go, inwardly stamping my feet with frustration.

Although this gentlemanly side to him was nice, I couldn't help feeling disappointed, and honestly, what was the point in holding out on me? We had kind of moved past all that. In fact, the whole date had been remarkably chaste. When he had suggested the pictures, I had been expecting the whole hand-up-my-skirt-in-the-back-row routine; I'd worn a skirt on purpose. Perhaps he was regretting rushing into it all, having brought it up so fast after his impromptu spanking that first Saturday. I didn't know, but I went to bed antsy and restless, wondering if this was all part of some elaborate game. He had said he wanted me begging for it, after all.

A week of flirty texts and long phone conversations followed but he made no more mention of kinky sex games, until I found myself blatantly contriving to bring it up in conversation. He deftly avoided all my attempts to do so, and soon I was crawling up the walls with frustration. I was distracted and grumpy at work, doodling absent-mindedly on my register in the weekly work meeting. I saw Margaret watching me with a baleful eye and sat to attention, but my thoughts were elsewhere.

'What if he's gone off me? Met someone else?' I wailed to Kim, insecurity kicking in when there was no offer of a date the following weekend.

He was bogged down with paperwork, apparently, and would make it up to me the weekend after. Of course I had agreed, and then inwardly cursed myself for not claiming that I myself would be busy. I didn't want these games; I had just got my head around the whole submissive scenario, had been hungry for it, almost, ready to delve further into this strange, secret world, and he had changed the rules on me. I couldn't help but think of Anna's comments about girls 'on the scene' who looked for new dominants. Perhaps he had found one more willing, who knew what she was doing? I chewed Kim's ears about it until she was rolling her eyes in exasperation.

'Why don't you just ask him? He's been in constant touch with you, hasn't he? I don't think he would bother if he was busy chaining someone else up to his cross.'

Typical Kim. I glared at her, while conceding she had a point. But I was too stubborn to 'just ask'. Not to mention reluctant to look so needy.

'I've never seen you like this over a guy, especially one you've just met,' she observed, scrutinising me.

I shrugged. 'I just don't like not knowing where I am,' I said lightly.

But inside, I had to admit Kim was right. I couldn't recall ever being so strung out over a guy. Especially one I hadn't even slept with. Kim was still eyeing me with suspicion.

'You've fallen for him,' she stated.

She leaned back against the bar, folding her arms and looking at me as if in triumph that she had figured it out. I shook my head vehemently.

'Don't be daft. I barely know him.'

'Hmmm.' She didn't believe me. In all honesty, I didn't believe me either. 'By the way,' she said, 'did Shane tell you about that new girl he's met? She's a tattoo model, apparently, so he's swanking around all over the place about it.'

Great. So if Alex disappeared, I couldn't even turn to Shane for comfort. I felt guilty at the thought even as I had it; he deserved to meet someone nice, not be my fall-back guy. I didn't want Shane, I wanted Alex. Bad.

I spent the weekend with Kim, hitting the cocktail bars on the Saturday, but no amount of glamming up or Sex on the Beaches or even hot young barmen took my mind off him. I texted him to tell him what a fabulous time we were, of course, having, and felt better at his reply.

Be good. No flirting. Or I shall spank you.

That sounded more promising. The hint of jealousy pleased me, especially after I had been so insecure all week. I showed Kim, grinning like the Cheshire Cat with a very big bowl of cream.

'That's good, right? He cares what I'm doing?'

She rolled her eyes at me, but it was with affection.

'You are lovesick.'

She was right, and it was ridiculous, really, how a simple text message could make so much difference. But then, I was still fighting to admit to myself the obvious: that, as Kim had pointed out, I was indeed falling for him. Whether this would have happened anyway, or whether I was experiencing the emotional bond peculiar to a certain type of relationship, as Anna had said, I didn't know and didn't much care. I just knew I didn't like the way it was making me feel: desperate, in every sense of the word. I longed for him.

If the lack of contact had been a calculated ploy on his part to make me crave him, it had certainly worked. I was on edge, my body strung out like an addict's for the next fix: raw with waiting, my every nerve singing with need.

And there was no sign yet of when that need would be sated.

Journal extract

It's been such a long week. I'm seeing Alex tonight – at last – but I feel awkward about it. I've spent so much time worrying and I've barely seen him. Work is manic, but I just can't get my head around anything but him at the minute. I need to snap out of it.

I wish I knew where, if anywhere, this is going. Things were so much easier before I met him . . . but who am I trying to kid? They were a lot more boring, too.

We have to have sex this weekend. Please, Lord . . .

Chapter Eleven

Ice skating. Just as it was coming up to mini-skirt weather, he wanted us to wrap up and go ice skating.

'With hindsight, I should have checked you had any sense of balance at all before I booked this,' he said drily, before we collapsed in another fit of giggles.

Yes, Alex was giggling again; I seemed to be having this effect on him during our dates. No doubt the sight of me falling unceremoniously on my backside was highly amusing. Although, as that had entailed him having to pick me up each time, pressing his body into mine, and eventually hold my hand around the rink, it hadn't necessarily proved to be a bad thing. As he stared down at me, eyes crinkled with laughter and our bodies crushed together, I had felt like a heroine in a chick flick, and handcuffs and crosses had never seemed so far away.

Back at my apartment we had finally stopped laughing and I drank in the sight of him, relaxed and sprawled over my sofa. He reached for my hand and pulled me down next to him, throwing an arm round me and bringing me into his body in one deft movement. His eyes had turned serious and they travelled slowly over my face before coming to rest at my mouth. I tipped my face to his, waiting for the press of his lips, but instead he gripped my chin, running his thumb over my waiting mouth.

'I've missed you.'

His voice was low. I blinked in surprise.

'I've missed *you*; I thought maybe you were having second thoughts.'

There, I had said it, admitted that I was already attached. I've never liked confessing my feelings but it was a relief to say it after two weeks of anxiety and desperate second-guessing.

'Hardly. I haven't stopped thinking about you.' He paused, as if considering his next words. 'I've been busy with work, both here and in Cyprus, and also I'm very close to finalising my divorce. I didn't want to be boring you with tales of legal wrangling. Once this is out of the way, we can move forward.'

'Oh?'

'If, of course, that's what you want? Another reason I've backed off a little . . . I want to be sure you're certain about this. You don't give very much away, Kelly. You're so sweet, so willing in the bedroom, but you play your cards very close to your chest out of it.'

I didn't know what to say to that. It seemed the time for some sweet nothings, but my inner slut was far too busy smirking at the 'sweet and willing' comment.

'I'm not playing games, Kelly.'

'Really?' – it was my turn to be serious – 'because I was beginning to think that's exactly what you were doing. I appreciate you've been busy, that's fine, but the way it's been so . . . intense, sexually, and then nothing. I didn't know what to think. Or feel.'

He ran a hand very lightly across my thigh. Even through the woolly leggings I had worn to go skating, his touch electrified every nerve, a stab of desire shooting through my groin as he stopped at the top of my leg and squeezed. It was meant to be a comforting gesture, judging by his next comment, but my body wasn't craving comfort.

'I'm sorry. I didn't want to drag you into my dealings with Frances, or to see you while I was preoccupied. You deserve my full attention. As did the end of my marriage.'

I looked at him, my lustful thoughts halting. I hadn't asked him about his wife – I was guessing that was Frances – as it hadn't felt appropriate this early on, and it hadn't occurred to me that he might be feeling raw about it. The idea made me feel uncomfortable, not to mention jealous. I had avoided thinking about the shadowy figure of his estranged wife, yet now here she was in the conversation, called up like an unwelcome spirit.

'Is everything going all right? With the divorce, I mean.'

'Oh, yes,' he nodded briskly, 'it will be signed and sealed in a matter of weeks, and it's all been fairly amicable. Unlike the marriage itself.'

'Do you want to talk about it?'

I tried not to sound too horrified. This new, more vulnerable side of Alex wrong-footed me. He smiled wryly, squeezing my leg again.

'There's little to say. We were, shall we say, incompatible.'

A thought struck me: 'Did she not share your tastes with you? In bed.'

'On the contrary. It was Frances who introduced me to the practice; she had had a brief relationship before me that had brought her into the scene and in turn she shared this with me. I was young, ready to explore, and infatuated, I suppose.'

I really didn't want to hear how infatuated he had been with his ex. Still, I was intrigued by the picture he was now painting for me, as well as surprised: she sounded perfect for him. He answered my thoughts as if I had spoken out loud.

'Frances was also a dominant, which made things a little trickier, of course. In the beginning, she professed to enjoy both sides, what people call a "switch", but as we got older it became clear that she was indeed, a natural top. And I am not' – he laughed – 'anyone's idea of a submissive.'

I could see that.

'So, it caused problems?'

'You could say so. Of course, there is far more to a good marriage than simply the sex, but Frances became more and more enamoured of the whole scene. We lived in London then, and frequented the clubs there.'

I frowned. He had told me he wasn't into the whole club thing.

'It wasn't really my preference,' he went on hurriedly, noticing the look on my face, 'but of course I wanted her to be happy. And in all honesty I had my own needs. So her suggestion was that we would play with other submissives together. It worked quite well, for a while.'

Oh, God. I so did not want to hear this. My stomach recoiled at the idea of Alex involved in some decadent threesome, or worse. I confess, I had been intrigued by the idea in the past, and if he were just a 'fuck buddy' it might even have excited me, but my immediate reaction to his words told me all I needed to know about how I felt for him. I wasn't willing to share him. With anyone. The very thought of him with someone else made me feel sick.

'So what went wrong?'

I was trying and failing to sound nonchalant, but I let out a sigh of relief at his next words.

'I believe in being monogamous, funnily enough. I'm not averse to some occasional fun, but for Frances it became much more than occasional. It became quite clear that I couldn't fulfil all her needs, and as I began to draw away from it all, she got more involved. Frances has a very deep-seated need to control, unfortunately, and my reluctance to take things as far as she wished to made her furious. We tried an open relationship for a while but it didn't work for me. I was brought up with very traditional views, where marriage is concerned.'

I smiled at that, thinking that Alex was very far from traditional, in my opinion. The conflict between his family values and his sexual needs must have been tough.

'So that's why you split up?'

'Eventually. I didn't want to divorce; it felt like a failure. On the surface, of course, we were a successful and well-off couple. Also I wanted children, but that wasn't happening. I spent the last few years of our marriage pretty much celibate, while Frances flaunted her ever younger and more submissive lovers in my face.' He paused at my shocked gasp. 'The more I withdrew from her, the more bitter she became. She fought the divorce at first, until I threatened to make her antics public, and then gave in.

As I said, it's progressed quite amicably since then. She's taken up with an older, richer man who no doubt indulges her proclivities.'

'She sounds like a total bitch,' I spat out, hating her, then instantly regretted my bluntness, but he chuckled at me, face softening.

'She is much damaged. But that part of my life is thankfully over.'

My heart ached for him then, at the lost look that crossed his face just for a fleeting minute as he recalled what were no doubt difficult memories. I squeezed his hand, not really knowing what to say, torn between compassion for him and a burning jealousy at his obviously sexually accomplished ex-wife.

'You don't miss it? The whole scene?'

He looked puzzled at my question.

'Well, it's still a part of my life, as you've experienced.'

I had to ask, even though I didn't want the answer: 'There have been others?'

He looked uncomfortable.

'I've had one or two flings since we split. But they were purely sexual; we didn't "date". There are girls who are happy to just play the role of submissive without getting any further involved.'

I wished I had never brought the subject up. A horrid thought struck me: 'Is that what you intended on doing with me?'

'No. I would never have suggested that to someone who worked under me. I would never have asked you for lunch that day.'

I had to wonder how someone went about finding a

submissive just for sex if they weren't going to date them. Did he order girls pre-wrapped online? I decided not to ask. In spite of my fascination, I had heard enough about his sexual past. And it had made me feel woefully inadequate. I couldn't put into words the sudden insecurity that was gripping me, and blurted out before I could stop myself: 'Why don't we go to the club? Where me and Kim went? Tomorrow night?'

As soon as I had said it, I convinced myself it was a good idea. I could be just as sexy as this Frances, I decided, and what was more I would be happy to play the submissive role that he wanted. Alex looked shocked, but nodded warily.

'If you like.'

I snuggled into him, running a fingernail down the side of his neck.

'I'll be all yours, all night,' I murmured in my best femme-fatale voice.

It worked, as he gripped my face with his hand and leaned down to claim my mouth again, kissing me with a passion that was almost hunger. I responded in kind. Two weeks of frustration and a need to release the new emotions he had awakened in me to the point of overflowing. I knew if he had wanted it, he could have had me there and then on the sofa. But he pulled back, kissing me on the forehead in a gesture that was becoming familiar.

'Thank you,' he said; then, when I looked confused, 'for understanding.'

It felt as though we had reached something important, though I wasn't sure what, but I nuzzled his face with a tenderness I hadn't felt before. He rose, lifting me up carefully, and I walked him to the door, already feeling the loss of him. He kissed me again before he left, softer this time, murmuring a goodbye.

'Tomorrow, beautiful.'

I watched him go down the stairs before shutting the door behind me and sighing like any smitten teenage girl. Then I remembered where we were going the next day and groaned to myself. What was I doing? Trying to outdo a woman I had never even met, who in any case sounded an absolute cow.

Before I had even sat back down, my phone beeped. Alex, with one of his blush-inducing texts.

Don't masturbate tonight. I'll see you tomorrow.

An order I had absolutely no intention of obeying . . .

Chapter Twelve

'You look amazing.'

I had gone all out: had my hair styled, my nails done, and I was wearing the tiny red bodycon I had considered for our first date, with fishnet hold-ups that allowed the ink work on my leg to show through, and killer heels courtesy of Kim. Slutty, perhaps – but then, that was the look I was going for.

I kept seeing Alex glance at me out of the corner of his eye as he drove, and his obvious admiration made me feel like a goddess. I had spent the day debating whether I should cancel the whole thing, but had decided it was too late for that; it had been my idea in the first place, after all. The fact that I had perhaps been hoping he would say no and would repeat his earlier line about preferring the privacy of his own bedroom I tried to push to the back of my mind . . .

Last night's revelations had given me plenty to think about. I felt I knew Alex better and had a deeper under-standing of why he ticked the way he did, but I also felt inexplicably jealous of the shadowy Frances. I sensed her lingering in the air between us, fuelling my insecure imagination. I had counselled female friends on this very subject before, but I just couldn't take my own advice about letting sleeping dogs – very much bitches, in this case – lie.

'Are you OK?'

He broke into my reverie, giving my knee a caress before letting go to change gear. I nodded in affirmation, as much to myself as to him. He gestured towards the glovebox.

'I have something in there for you.'

More nipple clamps? I opened the box, pulling out a small black velvet pouch. Reaching inside, I brought out a thin black leather band with studs. A collar. I looked over at Alex in surprise. He kept his eyes on the road, but there was that wicked smile tugging at the corners of his full mouth. Was this significant? I tried to remember how much I had told him of my conversations with Anna. I ran my fingers over the collar. It was small, delicate, not one of the scarier-looking contraptions I had spotted. Unassuming, really. Like a wedding band.

'This is to show I'm your sub?'

'It's not to make your dress look pretty, Kelly. Do you feel uncomfortable wearing it?'

I shook my head, reaching to put it on, and fumbling with it for a few moments until I realised it fastened at the back. I didn't feel uncomfortable; I felt claimed.

When we pulled up to the club he came round to help me out, as gentlemanly as ever, his eyes going straight to my crotch as I tugged down my dress.

'You're looking up my skirt,' I said accusingly.

'Indeed. No doubt that was the intention, given how short your dress is.'

I smiled.

'Not at all. I remembered you liked me in red. Whatever Sir wants, Sir must have.'

Alex looked down at me in amusement, and then brought his hand to the back of my neck, tugging at the nape so my head came back and I was staring straight into his eyes.

'You will call me Sir tonight, and with rather more respect. Understand?'

I swallowed, feeling the sensation I was now beginning to recognise, where the logical part of my mind wanted to argue against his demands, but something else, something deeper, made my belly twist and my legs weak. That feeling . . . It made me want to surrender my mind as my body already had, as soon as he voiced his commands.

'Yes, Sir,' I said demurely.

Let the games begin.

As before, it was the enthusiastic Marilyn who opened the door, this time in a different coloured fluffy jumper, but the obedient Kitty was nowhere to be seen. Marilyn recognised me instantly, enveloping me in a warm hug.

'I'm so glad you returned! And you must be Alex. Anna is around somewhere.'

As we stepped inside and our hostess bustled off, I looked quizzically at Alex.

'I rang ahead,' he explained. 'To arrange things.'

Arrange what? I regarded him with suspicion, but he was already steering me towards the bar. There was an edge to him tonight that I couldn't figure out; he seemed hyper-alert, almost poised for action. Wary, I thought. Although that worried me, it only added to his erotic power, giving his controlled, lithe movements a predator's air. He moved across the room, as always, as if he owned it. This was the Alex I had met, not the giggling charmer on the skating rink or the vulnerable jilted husband he had revealed himself to be the night before. I surreptitiously eyed him as we stood at the bar, trailing my eyes across his taut body clad in a black shirt – his only concession to the club dress code – and dark blue jeans that hugged his butt every time he moved. I had a sudden image of those muscles working, pumping in and out of me, and fought the urge to give him a good hard squeeze.

I wasn't the only one enamoured of Alex's charms; beside us at the bar a pretty blonde, who appeared to have come out in her underwear, was eyeing him lustily over her glass. Alex looked over at her and smiled politely, slipping an arm around my waist and drawing me in to him. The blonde looked disappointed as he turned away from her, and I couldn't resist a triumphant glance over his shoulder. The blonde glowered at me.

'I thought we could go upstairs for a while. I don't fancy hanging around here mingling all night. I have plans for you when we get home.'

'Isn't it a bit early? It won't be open,' I protested, my head whirling as I thought about what his 'plans' might entail. If we didn't have sex, I thought I might burst.

'It is for us. Come on.'

I followed him to the stairs, passing a group of exotically dressed young guys who eyed me as I went. Alex

paused to guide me in front of him, placing a hand posses-
sively on my waist.

'Am I allowed to ask what we're doing up here?' I
asked as I reached the landing. He guided me towards the
playroom.

'In here. You'll see.'

The playroom was empty, as I would have expected
since it was still barely past eight – except for one person,
resplendent in her best bad-bitch gear, hair tumbling in a
lush flame around her face. Anna.

I went to greet her, surprised, but Alex raised a hand to
hush me, stepping forward to kiss Anna on the cheek. I felt
a stab of jealousy. She looked beautiful, the very epitome
of a female dom. Like his wife? I tried to banish that
unknown face from my mind. Anna stepped towards me.
Her face was stern and unsmiling, though she did offer me
a quick wink, as if to reassure me it was fine; she was just
playing. She raised an eyebrow as she spotted the collar.

'It's official then? You're a good little sub now.'

I wasn't sure how to respond. She prompted me: 'Say
"Yes, Mistress."'

I looked over at Alex, glaring. I was damned if I was
calling another woman Mistress. He went over and shut
the door to the playroom, and I opened my mouth to
protest.

'It's just so we have some privacy.' He stepped over to
me, pulling me towards him, his eyes searching my face.
'You are OK with this? The same rules apply here, Kelly;
use the safe word anytime you want to.'

I nodded and Anna cut in, her voice more gentle now.

'You told Alex how much you enjoyed watching me

whip Kitty; he thought this might be a little treat for you. A reward.'

A thousand protests ran through my head, but none came out of my mouth. If this was what he wanted, I was reluctant to seem a prude after last night's revelations, and if I was totally honest with myself I was more than a little intrigued. It was only the idea of Alex looking at Anna that bothered me, but his eyes were, for the moment at least, firmly on me. As for Anna, she was a professional, wasn't she? I exhaled a long breath and looked at her, accepting the challenge, feeling my stomach twist with apprehension.

'OK.'

There was still no way I was calling her Mistress, and I was thankful when she didn't push the point, but instead motioned me forwards to the cross. It was bigger and more imposing than the one in Alex's room, but I guessed the principle was the same, and indeed there he was behind me, moving my arms and legs into position as Anna moved the cuffs into place around my wrists and ankles.

I felt the first stirrings of desire low in my body as he pushed my legs apart so that Anna could fasten them with the metal restraints. They bit into my skin a little, but if I didn't move too much I would be OK. Alex planted a kiss on my shoulder, then lifted my hair, trailing his lips across and up to the back of my neck. I felt him open his mouth, taking in the collar, before biting down hard on the back of my neck like a lion pinning his prey. The sensation sent a rush of pleasure down my spine and I jerked against my bonds, pushing myself into him.

'Mine,' he snarled, releasing me and stepping back.

Anna came forward then, running her manicured nails down my back and across the top of my buttocks through my dress, then down and over the backs of my thighs, across the gap of flesh between my dress and the hold-ups. It was such an unfamiliar sensation, but not unwelcome.

'Lift her skirt,' I heard Alex say, his voice thick with desire.

Anna complied, easing my dress up over my ass, exposing it in the tiny thong I had chosen, expecting that only Alex would be seeing it. But then, hadn't I had at least an inkling of something like this when I suggested the club in the first place? My thoughts were in chaos, and I had to wonder how the hell I had got myself into this. I buried my face into the cross to cover my embarrassment, but Anna tugged my head back up, lifting a flat, black paddle into my view.

'I'm going to hit you with this,' she purred, 'starting with ten times. I want you to count them out loud for me. Understood?'

I nodded my head yes, my mouth dry. I braced myself for the first blow, and when it came it was harsher than I expected from the look of the paddle, a hard strong slap across my ass that made me cry out.

'Count!' she snapped. Alex was silent, and I wished I could see his face.

'One,' I whispered weakly.

Anna tutted with impatience: 'Louder. We'll start again, and I'll repeat every blow that you forget to count, or that you don't count adequately.'

I could well see why Anna was a professional in her

field. I had got to know her a little and liked her, but this persona of hers was genuinely intimidating, if not down-right scary.

'One!' I shouted out as the paddle came down again, harder this time, shocking my skin. 'Two', as it came down again, and I sucked in my breath sharply.

There was no comforting rub or squeeze from Alex's hands in between strokes this time, and I thought I might well be safe wording before we got anywhere near ten. As if sensing my pain, Alex stepped round to the other side of me and stroked my hair.

'Take it, baby. You look so fucking beautiful.'

God help me, but I loved it when he said things like that. I moaned in response and he tugged at the top of my dress, pulling it down so my breasts swung free. Reaching in between my body and the leather he caught one breast in his hand, rolling and pinching the nipple in between his expert fingers as the next blow came down.

'Three,' I gasped, pushing myself forward into his hands, my body responding with such ease to his touch. His eyes burned into my mine and he continued to knead my breasts. 'Four . . . Five . . . Six . . .'

Alex stepped away. I sagged against the cross, welcom-ing the blows now, drifting off into that space Anna had spoken about, my breath shallow and my heart seeming to pump in time with the bass that throbbed through the ceiling from the bar below us. I smelled leather, and the musk of my own desire, and all my senses rolled up into one molten ball of heat low in my belly and groin.

'Nine . . .'

I arched my back, ready for the last blow, no longer

wanting her to stop, so that when I panted out the final 'Ten' I could hear the note of pleading in my voice.

'You want more?' Alex said, sounding pleased, the smug bastard.

'Yes, Sir.'

'Give her five more,' he murmured to Anna, who responded swiftly with a stronger slap than any of the others.

I didn't count this time and she didn't ask me to; she simply brought the paddle down in quick succession. I was panting like a dog when she had finished, a thin sheen of sweat covering my whole body. Anna stepped forward to release me, rubbing my wrists as she freed them from the cuffs, and only then did I realise how tightly they had been digging in. I would be bruised, again, in the morning. Anna looked pleased.

'She's good, isn't she? So responsive,' she said.

There was a brief pause, and then Alex's voice came, harsh and loud, startling me.

'Kiss her.'

I wasn't sure which one of us he was talking to, but my eyes widened as Anna tipped my face to hers, bringing her mouth to mine. She tasted and smelled both sweet and musky, her kiss soft and almost tentative, not the demanding intrusion I was used to from Alex's mouth. I kissed her back, my lips moving as if they had a will of their own, pressing my body into hers, my hand moving up to her hair of its own accord, the other going to her hip. I broke away breathlessly.

I was still half-naked from the paddling, my breasts exposed, and Anna reached for them, running her nails across the peaks until they stiffened beneath her touch. I was aware of Alex next to us; he had moved close enough that I could feel his hot breath ragged on my neck, but I kept my gaze on Anna. I didn't want to see what he was feeling, didn't want to break the spell of the moment. One thing I did know, even through the haze of my lust, was that if he made one move to touch Anna I was out of there. Fuck the safe word; I'd be gone. But he didn't move, just stayed there, poised, a hunter again.

Anna bent her head to my now-aching nipples, sucking one into her mouth in a swift movement that sent a burning shockwave straight to the damp heat between my thighs. I buried a hand in her hair, pulling her into me, a cry escaping my lips. I wanted this now, wanted her mouth on me.

And then Alex was there, gently but firmly separating us, his mouth set in a grim line, refusing to meet my eyes.

'That's enough.'

He pulled at my dress, and I wriggled back into it, my cheeks flaming as the realisation of what I had been about to do hit me. Anna stepped back, regaining her composure. She looked about to say something, but Alex was bundling me out of the door towards the stairs, dismissing her with a wave of his hand and a curt 'thank you'. Gripping my hand as if he thought I was about to run away, he all but pulled me down the stairs. I waved at a tipsy-looking Marilyn as we passed her in the hall, and she beamed at me, oblivious to our situation. Whatever that was.

'Goodbye, darlings. See you again soon.'

The cold air hit me as we got outside and I pulled my hand from Alex's grip as he advanced towards the car, throwing the door open for me.

'What's wrong? The whole thing with Anna – you set it up. Did I do something wrong?'

My voice caught on the last word as a horrible thought snaked into my mind. Had I not, somehow, been good enough? Alex stared at me a minute, then shook his head.

'Get in,' he said.

We drove back to his in silence, me stealing glances at him, but his eyes were firmly on the road, his body language forbidding. Confused, I turned my face to the window, fighting the sting of hot tears as they welled in my eyes. There was nothing more I could say.

Chapter Thirteen

We didn't speak for the entire journey back to his house, and the atmosphere in the car was tight with tension. I couldn't figure out what had gone wrong.

As we entered his house I put down the overnight bag I had brought, hoping to be finally staying for the whole night, and turned to Alex, trying to regain my composure. Before I had the chance to speak he had grabbed me by the arms, pushing me back against the wall and devouring my mouth with his. His body was rigid, his lips fierce and unyielding against mine. I sensed the anger in him and for a moment was panicked. His reaction, so utterly out of control and unexpected, frightened me even as his kiss and the crush of his body turned me on, fuelling the arousal he and Anna had already ignited. Torn between pushing him away to demand what was wrong and the growing urgency in his kiss, I went with the latter. I yielded, melding my body into his, opening my mouth under his persistence, opening my legs for him to press one thigh between them, burying my hands in his hair. He groaned into my mouth. He sounded tortured.

'Upstairs,' he said, and I knew where he meant.

We half-walked, half-fell up the stairs, grappling with each other's clothes in between kisses. His usual composure had vanished; his movements were fevered and rushed. He fumbled with the door to the playroom, pulling me in after him.

'Strip,' he ordered, shutting the door behind us. I wriggled out of my dress and knickers, only for him to nod too at my stocking-clad legs: 'All of it.'

I slid my hold-ups down and kicked off my shoes with more haste, watching as he went over to the drawers. He came back with what looked like a riding crop, and I blanched. I was already stinging from Anna and her innocent-looking paddle. He looked at me steadily, daring me to tell him no. I kept silent, holding his gaze, though my ass cheeks screamed at me in protest.

'Bend over,' he ordered, 'and touch your toes.'

I turned around, reaching down for my ankles, feeling horribly exposed in such a vulnerable position. Behind me, he slipped a hand between my legs, between moist lips, pinching my clit between thumb and forefinger. It was a different, but pleasurable, sensation. I heard him slap the crop against his palm. It sounded vicious.

'Ready?'

No, I most certainly was not. Still, I answered him, gave him what he wanted to hear, knowing I was testing the edge of my own limits.

'Yes, Sir.'

'Good girl.'

The crop whisked through the air and came down hard across my already-sore ass. I yelped, and it was all pain.

Once more, then again, and then, thank God, I heard him throw the crop down. He kneeled down behind me and laid soft butterfly kisses on my outraged cheeks. Tears sprang to my eyes at the tender, intimate gesture, and then I felt moisture of an altogether different nature as he laid the same fluttery touch over my labia where they peeped between my thighs.

'I don't ever,' he said, low enough that I had to strain to hear him, 'want to see you touch anyone else ever again.'

It was your idea, I protested in my mind, but decided this wasn't the time to discuss it. The blood was rushing to my head from bending over, and I shifted from one foot to the other. He got up in an abrupt movement.

'Sit on the bed, and open your legs.'

I got up, grateful for the release, and sat down on the soft bed, parting my thighs for him so that I was naked to his gaze. He let his eyes travel over me in that languorous way of his. He had regained his composure now and leaned back against the wall, letting his gaze come to rest between my legs.

'Wider. Good. Now touch yourself. Just one finger, that's right, just on the tip of your clit. Now put it inside you . . . and another. Good. Now suck them. Suck your fingers.'

I tasted my own juices, salt and tang and musk, squirming under his scrutiny, but not wanting him to stop his demands. I had never touched myself in front of a lover like this before. During intercourse, maybe, but not for their private viewing pleasure. I was getting accustomed to doing things with Alex that were new to me. The look on his face turned me on past the point of any embarrassment, and I sucked my fingers slowly, in and out of my mouth, staring straight into his eyes.

'Quite the little exhibitionist, aren't you? Now rub your clit again, harder. Make yourself come.'

I obeyed with eagerness, my pussy wet and greedy around my fingers, leaning back on one elbow and tipping my head back, giving in to the sensations. I was close, so close, by the time Alex ordered me to stop that I would have carried on for just a second, just enough to tip myself over the edge, but he was there above me, slapping my hand away.

'Greedy girl.'

'Please, Alex, Sir . . .'

My voice sounded slurred, incoherent with want. He smiled and leaned over me so that I thought he was about to kiss me, but instead he was reaching for something above my head. The restraints.

'Put your arms back. These are soft; they won't bite into your skin like the cuffs.'

He tied the silky restraints carefully. They were attached to black pieces of fabric that reached out from under the bed. From what I could remember of the set-up here, there were two more at the bottom of the bed for my ankles. And indeed he was moving down and spreading my legs to fasten them. I was completely helpless, spread-eagled underneath him.

'Did you bring your gifts?'

I wondered what he meant, then remembered the blindfold and clamps. It seemed so long ago now since he had given me them.

'They're downstairs. In my bag,' I managed.

My whole body ached with the need for the orgasm he had interrupted, my clit so oversensitive it hurt. The pain in my buttocks had faded by comparison. He went and came back quickly, his footsteps swift on the stairs, the blindfold in his hand.

'I think we had best leave the clamps for tonight. I think you've had enough testing of your pain tolerance. I don't want you to crash.'

'Crash?'

Of course, he was talking about the endorphin rush Anna had mentioned. I gulped as he fastened the blindfold around my head and the room went dark. I felt vulnerable as he moved away, unable to see him, unable to move, every sense heightened, every nerve raw.

'Alex?'

Then I felt him, his hot breath against my thigh, against my pussy. He gave a long slow lick along my cleft, making me wriggle against my bonds, and then went back to my thighs, nipping, sucking, and then nuzzling my pussy, kissing me as if it were my mouth. The soft, deliciously erotic sensation was too much; I felt myself cresting, then the waves of my orgasm crashed through me as he sucked my clit into his mouth, suckling on it as the orgasm rode me harder and longer than I had ever experienced. I thrashed on the bed, the restrictions to my movement making me more frantic, only vaguely aware that I was screaming his name.

He kept his mouth on me until the sensation calmed, kissing all around my labia as if he meant to soothe me, then moving up to my torso, stroking my hair and my breasts. My hair was damp around my face.

'You beautiful, sexy bitch,' he breathed into my ear as he leaned over me, tugging at a lobe.

'God, Alex that was amazing.'

Such an understatement: I didn't have the words for what he had just done to me. The aftershocks of my orgasm still ran through me, my ass cheeks still throbbed, but in a way that now only added to the pleasure in the rest of my body.

'Oh, we're far from done yet.'

His hand was back at my thighs, cupping my whole pussy. I was drenched, could feel it on my thighs and the quilt beneath me, and as he slid his fingers into me I accepted them greedily, clenching around them as he slid them deeper and found the raised sweet spot on the front wall, flickering expertly in a come-hither motion. Incredibly, I felt another orgasm build, a deeper, tighter sensation that contracted deep inside me. He slid another finger in, then another, stretching me slightly, still working that spot, his thumb circling my clit in a light motion, mindful of my sensitivity after the first orgasm. He had such an expert touch. I felt like clay in his hands, ready to be modelled by him. I couldn't even touch myself like this. The inside of my pussy swelled and throbbed until I had an acute urge to pee. I wriggled away, or tried to, held captive as I was, but he steadied me with a hand low on my belly.

'It's all right, sweetheart. Relax.'

'I need the toilet,' I said, mortified. His hand pressing on my stomach was making the sensation worse, even as I could feel my climax building to breaking point.

'No, you don't. It will pass, trust me. Just relax.'

I tried, making a conscious effort to deepen my breathing and let go of the tightness in my belly. My pussy continued to swell and contract around his hand as if my body were trying to expel his fingers from inside me, and I moaned, begging for release. His thumb pressed harder on my clitoris and he moved his hand out of me in one smooth motion, and I was screaming again as another orgasm racked me. And that wasn't all: I gushed. There was no other word for it. My orgasm gushed out of me in a flood of sensation and liquid that left my thighs and the bed drenched.

Having been bucking against the restraints, I collapsed back against the bed. He reached up and pulled the blindfold off, and I gazed up at him in wonder.

'What the hell was that?'

'You ejaculated. It's never happened before?'

I shook my head, flushing until I saw the look of delight in his face. He kissed me with his tongue deep in my mouth, then broke away and began to free me from the ties. I was shaking, and went to sit up, to reach for him, but he pulled me into his arms.

'It was my plan to fuck you now, but I think you've had enough. I'll run you a bath, order us some food. You need to eat.'

I nodded, disappointed. He saw my face and chuckled.

'Don't worry, we've got all night. You are staying?'

'I'd love to. But Alex, about earlier—'

He lifted a hand to stop me.

'We'll talk later. I made an error in judgment earlier, I believe. About myself, as much as you.'

I frowned, not understanding, but he was off into the

bathroom, calling me over his shoulder. I followed wearily, feeling tired now. A hot bath and food was well in order, to say the least.

As he ran the bath I inspected myself in the mirror. I was still wearing the collar, and with my hair in disarray and face flushed, lips plump and eyes lazy from pleasure, I looked wanton. Alex came up behind me, locking gazes with me in the glass.

'You really are very beautiful. But I'm sure you've been told that before.'

'Not really.'

I ducked my head, breaking the stare. I'm not very good with compliments. He reached underneath my hair to unfasten my collar.

'It seems a shame to take this off. You look ridiculously horny in it. Especially blindfolded and bound.'

I stepped into the bath, a luxurious corner spa with bubbling jets. The water was warm velvet on my skin, caressing my tender flesh. Only as I sank down and lay back, cocooned in white froth, did I realise how much the night had taken out of me, physically and emotionally. I was aching in places that I didn't know could ache.

'I'll order us some food.'

He disappeared downstairs and I heard him on the phone, ordering for me without bothering to ask what I wanted, but I was too tired and dreamy to grumble. He was back in minutes. I reached a hand out to him, all of a sudden vulnerable and wanting him near me.

'Get in?' I asked, thinking not of sex, but comfort.

Still, as he undressed in front of me my thoughts turned inevitably to the former. I had had little chance to really look at him fully naked until now, and I made no secret of devouring his body with my eyes. Tall and broad, rather lithe and toned, he was perfect. I dropped my gaze to his groin and was rewarded by the sight of him swelling under the scrutiny. He dropped down into the water, and I tutted at him.

'I was enjoying the view.'

He lifted my legs in between his, resting my feet on his chest, caressing them. I jerked a foot away as he pressed into the sole with his thumb.

'I hate the underside of my feet being touched,' I explained.

'It's a sensitive area. Some people love it, however; there's a practice known as bastinado, centuries old, where the soles of the feet are lightly whipped.'

I grimaced.

'Well, don't ever bother trying that with me. I'll safe word before you know it.'

He roared with laughter.

'I've caned you, tied you up, had you whipped in a public place and spanked the hell out of you, yet you only threaten to safe word when I touch your feet? You are refreshing. If a little weird.'

I pretended to kick him, though I was chuckling myself. I sank further into the water, closing my eyes.

'This feels so good. I love being in the water.'

'We have a heated pool at the family home in Cyprus. You'll love it. Perhaps you can join me next time I have to go over.'

My eyes flew open, but his own were closed now, his hands massaging my calves. I wasn't sure what to say. Did he mean it, or was it just an off-the-cuff comment?

His hands moved up to my lower thighs, pulling me towards him, circling and kneading with a growing intensity. Feeling bold, I reached for him under the bubbles, finding him rock hard. He kept his eyes closed as I squeezed and massaged his cock in time with the motion of his hands on my legs, but I could feel the reaction in his body, his cock swelling further in my hand. He made no attempt to order me or take charge of the situation, just lay there, totally relaxed except for his pulsing shaft.

'I want you inside me . . . Sir.'

My voice was thick. His eyes opened.

'You greedy girl.'

He stood up then, reaching for me.

'On your knees, baby.'

I knelt up, warm water cascading down my chest and back, and took him in my hand again, running my lips over the swollen head of his cock, then sucking just over the tip. He shuddered, bending a little to reach my swaying breasts with one hand, rubbing the soapy bubbles into me. I arched into his hands, amazed at my immediate response to him even after he had played my body so thoroughly already. I slid him into my mouth until I felt him reach the back of my throat, paused and slid him deeper still. He stayed very still and made no move to pull my hair or dominate me as he had in the car, just let me take my time and relax until I had slid him right into my throat, and back to the tip, and then right down again. A few more strokes and he groaned as if tortured.

'Baby, stop. I don't want to come yet.'

I stopped and moved my attention to his balls, high and tight against his body in spite of the heat. I drew one gently into my mouth, enjoying the feeling of his most vulnerable flesh on my tongue, feeling for once as though I were the powerful one. He guided me up by my shoulders, kissing me long and deep, our wet bodies pressed together. I could feel the heat curling in my body again, melting me. He grabbed my chin in his hand and opened his mouth to say something, his eyes serious, when the sound of the doorbell jarred into my consciousness.

'Food.'

He got out of the bath, throwing on a black towelling robe, and handing me a towel. As I stepped out, a sudden chill hit me. He looked at me in concern.

'You need to eat. I should have taken care of that earlier. Let me go and sort this – there's a spare robe in my bedroom.'

It was the first time I had actually set foot in his bedroom. The real one, not the 'playroom'. Like the rest of the house, it was luxurious, yet at the same time spare. Unlike my flat, which had my personality stamped all over it – or at least that was my excuse to avoid the housework. I was betting he had a cleaner.

He bounded back up the stairs, handing me a plate of sweet-smelling curry.

'You like curry?'

'I love it. Just as well, really.'

'Don't be sarcastic. Eat.'

I tucked in gratefully, curling my legs up beneath me on the bed. No formal dinner at the table this time. I relaxed back into the big pillows, feeling completely at home. Yet another kind of barrier had been broken tonight, another bridge crossed, though as usual I couldn't explain how or why. The club, and Anna, seemed a world away.

Yet he chose just that moment to bring it up. I had just set my plate down and taken a big gulp of water when he spoke. He had barely touched his own food.

'I couldn't stand watching you with Anna earlier. It was erotic, of course, but wrong on so many levels.'

I was puzzled.

'Then why do it? You had arranged it before we even got there, hadn't you?'

Now Alex was the one who looked puzzled.

'But I thought it was what you wanted? You wanted to go there, you suggested it last night – seemed very eager, in fact. After everything I told you about my marriage, about the things we did, and then you came out with that . . . well, I assumed the idea excited you.'

I shook my head. I had screwed up big time.

'Then why suggest it?'

Miserably, I admitted, 'I thought it was what you wanted. You told me all that stuff about you and her, and I know I'm not very experienced at this, and I wanted to, I don't know, I thought you might miss all that and I was worried I might not be' – oh, God, this was embarrassing, my words were coming out in a rush – 'enough. Compared to what you had.'

Alex's expression ran through the whole spectrum from amused to angry before he settled for baffled.

'Are you a crazy woman? Did you listen to anything I said?' He shook his head. 'I've gone about this all wrong, haven't I? I got carried away far too soon, didn't properly explain things.' He waved his hands in the air. 'That first night, I should never have just walked out and left you; one of the first things you learn as a dominant is the importance of taking care of your sub after any play. I've confused the issue, trying to date you properly, but I'm not looking for a purely sexual arrangement, or I would have gone about this entirely differently. Neither do I want the horror that my marriage became. Kelly, what do you want from me?'

I blinked. Shouldn't I be asking him that? Wrong-footed, I blurted out the simple truth: 'You. What else?'

He took a deep breath as if relieved, I thought. His next words were unexpected, but the minute he said them I knew they were the very words that I had wanted to hear for weeks now.

'I'm falling for you. Falling in love with you. It's not an excuse for the way I behaved initially, but even from the beginning I sensed this was different. I hadn't planned on this, but it appears to have happened anyway.'

I laughed, delighted. He looked offended, and I hurried to explain myself, struggling to stop myself whooping in triumph. Far from his protestations of love scaring me, I felt a giddy excitement.

'Who does plan on it, ever? But I feel the same, Alex. I hated how much I missed you the past two weeks, and all this . . . the sex part, is amazing, I've never been so turned on, but it goes deeper than that. I honestly don't think I would be able to do this, let you do all this to me, if it wasn't more than just physical.'

But his next words cut me to the quick.

'It's common for a submissive to feel attached to her dom, especially if they're new to the practice.'

I pouted, annoyed for a moment that he was trying to categorise my feelings for him.

'It's not that. You know it's not.'

He looked suddenly, and uncharacteristically, vulnerable. I leaned over, nearly knocking the plate, and kissed him. He was hesitant, and I kissed him more forcefully until he responded in his typical way by pushing me back on the bed, pinning my arms and crushing my lips with his. My robe fell open, and he ran a hand down my body, pushing my thighs open. He raised himself up on one elbow, a question in his eyes.

'Yes,' I said simply.

And so, after weeks of agonised questioning and waiting, we had sex. I know, I know, after the immense build-up there should have been more fireworks, but I was already spent, and Alex no doubt wound up to breaking point. It was quick, and intense, and though I didn't orgasm again, I felt content. I fell asleep in his arms afterwards, after we whispered, for the first time, 'I love you' to each other. Just like a regular, standard relationship. As far as I was concerned, it couldn't have been more perfect.

As I drifted off to sleep, I thought of how vulnerable he had looked when he admitted his feelings, how angry his earlier jealousy had made him, and I remembered Anna's words: 'The submissive has the real power; the dominant can never truly let go, not without her permission.' I fell asleep smiling. Finally, I felt he was mine as much as I was his.

Chapter Fourteen

We had sex again in the morning, Alex having resumed his authority. He woke me with an insistent erection in the small of my back, his hand twisting and pulling at my nipples. I arched my ass into him even as I adjusted to being awake.

'Morning, beautiful.'

I rolled over, reaching for his cock, but he slapped my hand away.

'You're not getting away with things so easily today. Turn on to your front, on your knees, with your face in the pillow.'

'Alex . . .'

'Do it.'

What the hell. I did as instructed, then lifted my head – as instead of touching me he went off into the other room with a curt 'stay there'. He returned with silk ties. Now what was he up to?

'Put your arms down so your wrists are by your ankles. I'm going to tie them together, then fuck you with your arse in the air and your face down, like a good little slut.'

If I had thought declarations of love meant a more vanilla sex life I had clearly been wrong. I realised that I was glad – hell, more than glad – and lay still as he tied my hands near my feet, leaving me trussed up and open to him, ass in the air, laid bare and exposed.

He ran his hands over my cheeks and they throbbed in return, a reminder of the punishment they had endured the night before. Alex began gently rubbing a fingertip up and down the exposed slit peeking between my thighs, going higher each time so that his finger toyed with my asshole on the upstroke. He leaned close, his breath hot on my thighs, kissing the sore skin of my butt cheeks. I knew without looking that I was bruised but I couldn't move; if I even turned my head too far I was in danger of toppling over. I could only lie where he had tied me, hands at my ankles, face in the pillow, ass and pussy at the mercy of his ministrations.

I heard him rummaging for something, heard the slither and snap of a condom, and then felt a cold, oily liquid running down my cleft. He slid into me while I was still tight and unprepared, making me gasp with the thickness of him, my insides contracting round his shaft like a velvet glove. He moved slow and deep so that I felt every inch of him, felt myself open up and become lubricated with my own arousal.

'You feel so good inside me,' I moaned.

It was amazing being able to savour the sensation after the exhaustion of the night before. Trapped in position as I was, every movement was that bit more intense as I gave myself up to him, my intimate parts on display like a crude offering.

I tried to move my head to one side as my neck grew stiff and he grabbed my hair at the nape of my neck with one hand and moved it for me, giving a vicious little tug as he did so, before slamming into me harder, right up to his crotch, until I felt his balls pressing against me. His hand moved over my buttocks, kneading and circling closer to the centre until his thumb pressed against the opening. I tensed, unused to being touched there. It felt odd, but the newness of it aroused me further. Using the added lubricant, he eased his thumb into me, working it slowly inside me. I felt invaded at first, but then, as I grew accustomed to the sensation, I found that it added a wickedly dirty edge to the feel of him inside me.

'I want to fuck your ass,' he gasped, and my heart pounded at the illicit idea. 'Not today, not while you're still sore, but soon. I'm going to fuck your ass while I work my hand, then a toy, inside your pussy. I'm going to fill you up until you can't take any more.'

My pussy clenched in a spasm of desire around him at his words, and as it did so he pushed another finger into my ass, probing and twisting in time with the rhythm of his cock inside me. I tried to rock back against him but my position prevented me from moving more than a centimetre or so and I groaned in frustration, wanting him deeper and faster. To finally have him inside me felt so good but so frustrating, being as I was unable to see or touch him or participate in any way other than lying there and letting myself be taken.

He moved the hand that was playing with my ass to my hip, gripping me as he rode me faster, giving me what I craved. Then he reached around with his other hand for my now waiting clit, deftly circling it with the tip of his finger.

'Come for me, baby. Let me hear you.'

My hands strained against the ties, settling for holding on to my own feet as I tried to push myself against his hand, his touch bringing me to the edge of release then leaving me begging as he reduced the pressure.

'Alex, Sir, please, let me come,' I implored, almost mewing in frustration, knowing it was what he wanted.

He sped up the rhythm of his strokes but kept his touch on my clit butterfly-light until I was whimpering with need, then gave a few last fevered thrusts, rubbing my clit in earnest and pushing a finger back into my ass. The orgasm hit me just as I felt his cock twitch and he began to pump his own climax into me, and I screamed his name into the pillow, the lack of movement that my position allowed only adding to the intensity of my release.

'Oh, fuck, yes.' He collapsed over my back, spent and sweaty.

We lay there momentarily, our breaths fierce and fast as our pulse rates recovered, and I slowly became aware of the painful throbbing in my limbs. My wrists ached, too.

'Can I get up now, please, Sir?' I eventually said.

My breath came in gasps as he released me from my tight bonds, pulling me into his arms as I sat up and stretched my cramped legs. I gave him a grin as he squeezed me tight, and was taken aback when he covered me in kisses. He kissed my mouth, my nose, eyelids and forehead, his eyes hot and searching as they found mine. He looked rumpled and boyish. And very, very fuckable.

'Are we doing this?'

I looked puzzled. Hadn't we just 'done' this, and very, very satisfyingly?

He went on, his face as serious as his sentiment: 'Me. You. Giving it a proper go.' He waved his hand as if that explained everything.

It was everything I had hoped for. I smiled, wriggling further into his arms.

'Yes, Alex. Yes, let's do this.'

This was one offer I was more than ready to submit to.

Journal extract

Whooo! Finally had sex. I've never waited so long to go all the way; talk about prolonging the foreplay. And he loves me! It felt so good to finally admit how I feel about him.

It would have been a perfect weekend, apart from the whole kissing-Anna-at-the-club thing. It got us talking, felt like a watershed of sorts, and now we're actually properly 'together', so I suppose all's well that ends well and all that.

I wonder if it will change things, being a 'proper' couple. I guess I'll find out soon enough . . .

Chapter Fifteen

So there it was, we were now officially together. Boyfriend and girlfriend, or, as Alex preferred it, 'partners'. When he dropped me back at mine on the Sunday night, he handed me my new collar.

'You forgot this.'

I smiled, fingering the black leather.

'Should I wear it to work tomorrow?' I lifted it to my neck and batted my eyelashes at him. He laughed before warning me: 'Don't say too much at work.'

'Does it matter? It's not illegal for us to be dating.'

I didn't like the idea of us being a secret, and wondered for a horrible moment if he was having second thoughts about taking things further. He had been unconcerned before about picking me up from work; I remembered his cheeky wave at Margaret the day of the impromptu blowjob.

'No, of course not, but I don't want you to be the subject of gossip, or for it to put you in a compromising situation; if you went for a promotion, for instance.'

I snorted with derision at the idea of Margaret ever considering me for promotion, even besides the fact that

I'd be unlikely to apply; moving up within Adult Ed would only mean more paperwork and less time with the students, which was the only part I enjoyed. Still, I recognised the logic of what he was saying.

'OK, if anyone should ask, I'll just say I'm your sex slave, and you enjoy tying me up and spanking me of a weekend,' I chirped as I ran up the stairs to my door, hearing Alex laugh before he drove off.

When I got in, I threw myself on the sofa and lay there for a while, mulling over the weekend's events, a silly schoolgirl grin firmly in place. It wasn't just the amazing sex that had put it there. For it occurred to me that we were now together and in love, like any vanilla couple. Perhaps it would be easier for me to accept the sexual desires he had unleashed in me now that I had the framework of a more standard relationship to indulge them in. The silly grin lasted all the next day – in fact, most of the week. I even caught myself singing as I handed out marked essays, which earned me more than a few bemused looks from my students.

The following Friday we went to an upmarket wine bar over Alex's side of town; the kind of place where a cocktail cost as much as my weekly food shop. I raised my eyebrows when the waitress brought over a bottle of Champagne.

'To us,' Alex announced, pouring the drinks and lifting his own in a toast. 'I thought we should celebrate.'

I toasted him back and sipped my drink, enjoying the tingle of the bubbles on my tongue. I could get used to this. I looked over the menu, screwing my face up at some of the dishes on offer.

'Pigs' cheeks? Ewww.'

'They're a delicacy.'

'I'll stick with steak,' I said firmly.

Alex shook his head in amusement at my unrefined taste. He ordered lobster.

'So,' he asked, as I struggled to cut up my meat, trying not to send peas flying everywhere, 'how are you feeling about things?'

I looked at him quizzically.

'About us? Fantastic. You're not' – and the thought made my chest constrict with a fleeting panic – 'having second thoughts?'

'Of course not. I've never been so certain about anything. I'm just making sure this hasn't, ah, altered things in the bedroom?'

I was relieved he had mentioned it. I had been thinking the same thing myself. Could I be his submissive and his girlfriend? I could certainly give it my best shot.

I gazed at him with what I hoped was a lustful look and lowered my voice.

'I was assuming things would be much the same . . . Sir.'

The smile he gave me was deliciously dirty.

Which is how I felt a few weeks after we had finally consummated our relationship, as I knelt face down on the floor of his study while he sat in front of his desk watching me impassively. He hadn't spoken for at least five minutes, although it felt like hours. The excitement of not knowing what he had planned had my breath coming in shallow beats and my nipples stiffening as they brushed against the cold laminate floor. I was naked, clad only in thigh-high boots and my collar.

'Do you want to come to me, slut?'

I sucked in a sharp breath, raising my head to nod.

'Yes, Sir.'

'Then come. On your hands and knees. Crawl to me, baby, and do it slow.'

This was new, and I hesitated, uncertain. It felt like yet another level of submitting; it was one thing to allow him to do as he wanted but to do this, to go to him in blatant submission, was another thing entirely. I swallowed, unsure how to react, my heart racing. He spoke again, his voice low and beguiling.

'Come on, baby, you can do this.'

My body felt unwilling to move as I lifted my torso on to my hands, my cheeks burning as I made to move towards him, looking up at him. He tutted.

'Keep your head down and keep your back arched as you move. Let me see that gorgeous body of yours.'

Spurred on by his compliments, I made my way over to him, keeping my gaze to the floor in willing servility but arching my back and stretching my body to give my movements a sensual sway. I sneaked a peek at him through my lashes and smiled to myself in triumph as I saw his eyes glaze over with lust. I went to him even slower than was necessary, prolonging his own anticipation as if in some small revenge for the long moments I had spent face down and ass up on the cold study floor.

As I neared him, I heard the unmistakable sound of his zipper lowering and my mouth moistened in readiness. I had come to love taking him in my mouth and was becoming adept at taking him deeper and moving my lips, tongue and throat in a way that had him groaning out my name. The taste and smell of him was enough to tighten my pussy with need. But as I reached and automatically went to fellate him, he held me off, lifting my face by my chin to look at him so that I sat back on my haunches. His cock sprang up thick and ready and he touched himself with one hand, moving the other to my breasts. He fondled me gently before giving each nipple a quick and vicious tug.

Then he reached for the butterfly clamps that I only now realised were on his desk. Of course, before he had ordered me in here all but naked he would have known how he wanted to play it. I licked my suddenly dry lips as I saw the clamps in his hands. I had wondered when they were going to make an appearance. Lately his nipple play had been getting rougher and more prolonged, as if in readiness for more brutal treatment. He would twist and pinch until my breasts ached. I had such sensitive nipples they practically had a direct line to my clit, so I guessed he had been building me up to the clamps.

'This won't hurt, but they will pinch a little. It's when you take them off that they will really throb, but,' he paused to suck a thumb and forefinger and then teased one nipple with them until it stood to stiff attention, 'by that point, you'll love it.'

I hoped he was right, wincing as he fastened the clamp over me. After the initial pinch it wasn't too bad, and my arousal increased as he carefully applied the second.

'Gorgeous.' He admired his handiwork. 'And now, you may suck my cock.'

I bent my head to take him into my mouth, swirling my tongue around his glans to lubricate it before sucking it vigorously, then slowly sliding down the length of his shaft. As I did so he tugged and twisted on the clamps, pulling my breasts up and sending shocks of pleasure through my nipples and down to my now-throbbing clit. As I sucked him harder he pulled harder, so that I moaned around his cock.

Abruptly he stood up, taking me by surprise.

'Stand up and turn around. Bend over the desk with your palms flat on it. Yes, like that.'

He kicked my legs wider apart with his foot as I bent over just enough to support my weight on my outstretched hands, the stiletto boots putting me at just the right height. He reached around to my breasts with one hand, pulling at each of the clamps in turn as he eased his cock into me, his girth making me gasp. He began to move inside me, slow and rhythmic, teasing at my nipples. It was an exquisite torture that made me desperate for more, but every time I tried to push my ass into him, hungry for him, he only slowed down, making me grip the desk with my fingers in frustration. I was desperate to touch myself, but knew I would only be reprimanded and that he might even stop altogether, so I tried to hold myself still, the sensations building in me as he played my body expertly. I was so wet around him I could feel my juices soaking my thighs, and a high whimpering sound came unbidden from my mouth.

'You like that, baby? Hmm, I think I'm being too soft on you.'

He pounded into me then with a stroke that all but had me sprawling over the desk, stopped only by his hand in front giving a now-truly-vicious twist to my aching breasts. He fucked me hard and fast for a while, his hands at my breasts mimicking his rhythm, and I drowned in the pain then pleasure then pain then pleasure that warred for supremacy within me until they merged into one and I was no longer aware of the difference between them.

He stopped, pulling me up and round and on top of him so that I was straddling him on his chair, and paused for a moment to remove the clamps, tossing them to one side. As promised my nipples began to throb immediately and with an intensity that made me gasp. He took my breasts in his hands, pushing them together and sucking hard on my already tortured nipples. I rode him frantically, my orgasm taking me over completely, his mouth sending shockwave after shockwave through me, drawing my orgasm out as if he were wringing every last drop out of me. Only when I collapsed on top of him, panting, did he release my breasts, guiding me back on to my knees in front of him to finish as we had begun.

I can, without hesitation, thoroughly recommend nipple clamps.

They weren't the only toy Alex introduced me to. The next week he took me shopping to a very exclusive shop full of expensive lingerie and home to another, partly obscured, room full of things that made me blush. I was a modern girl – I owned a vibrator and discussed their relative merits with my friends – but this was something else.

A dazzling array of restraints, cuffs, whips, paddles and floggers confronted me, running the gamut from fluffy pink ticklers to menacing black floggers with cruel spiked tips. The paddles designed to leave patterns or words such as 'love', 'sexy 'or 'bitch' intrigued me. I imagined the wielder would need a very precise aim to bring the paddle down in exactly the same spot each time, leaving the word or pattern emblazoned in your flesh. I wondered if it were possible to get your own made; I quite liked the idea of being 'branded' with Alex's name or a word of our own. I turned to show him the paddles, and saw him fingering a pair of white circular pads with leads.

'What are they?'

I leaned over his shoulder to look. He held them up for me.

'They go on your nipples. It's electro-sex: they give you little shocks—'

I waved my hand, having heard quite enough. Alex chuckled.

'I think you might enjoy them, after your reaction to those clamps. Maybe another time.'

I shook my head and wandered off to look at the vibrators, an area I was much more comfortable with. I frowned at a bulbous-looking glass dildo with ridges, wondering exactly what it was designed for. The shape struck me as strange. I went over for a closer look, then blushed as I picked it up and realised what it was. An anal plug. I turned it over in my hand, intrigued in spite of myself.

'You like it?' Alex came up behind me, making me startle. 'We'll get it.'

He whipped it out of my hand before I could protest. Not that I was about to; we hadn't yet tried anal sex. I had never been sure I wanted to, but the pleasure I had got from him using his fingers there that first morning, and since, had left me eager for further exploration.

After grimacing at the pinwheels and skin hooks I wandered down to look at the underwear. Being with Alex had renewed my love of sexy lingerie, though the PVC stockings I had bought the previous week in an attempt to look the part had left me with sweaty, itchy legs, and took ages to get on and off. The trick, Alex had told me as he joined in the struggle to peel them from my legs, was to pop some talcum powder in them first.

Alex was heading towards the till, glass dildo in hand as well as a selection of thin black ropes. A thrill went through me as I speculated as to what his plans were with those. I linked my arm through his as we left the shop, and he dropped a tender kiss on my forehead before opening the door. It was a sweet, romantic gesture and I smiled to myself as I slid into the passenger seat, acknowledging how it now felt perfectly natural to find something romantic in the middle of shopping for butt plugs.

We sat in my local park together later that week, relaxing in the warmth of the summer sun, Alex looking too hot for his own good in boyish cut-offs and a tight white T-shirt that emphasised his natural tan. I had thrown a picnic together. It had been my idea; as much as I loved the fancy restaurants and wine bars he took me to, I wanted to bring him into my life a little, too. He seemed perfectly at ease. He had even wanted to throw bread to the ducks.

He sat on the grass and I lay, head in his lap, while he stroked my hair.

'This is nice,' he commented. 'Just you and me in the sun. We should have a holiday soon.'

'You must hate the weather here,' I mused, 'compared to when you go back to Cyprus.'

'Yes. But there are a few things that make it more pleasant.'

He leaned down to kiss me and I tipped my face to his, but our embrace was disturbed by the sound of his phone trilling away in his pocket. He sighed and sat up, then, when he looked at the screen, pushed me gently off his lap, standing up to answer it. I propped myself up on one elbow to look at him.

'Mama,' he answered, his voice warm.

I lay back down, watching him as he walked a little way off. I turned my face back to the sun, enjoying its warmth, Alex's voice a low murmur in the background. I couldn't make out what he was saying other than a few snatched words. Then I heard one that made me sit back up.

'. . . Frances . . .'

He was talking about his wife? In spite of myself, feeling guilty for listening, I strained to make out the rest of his conversation, but he had moved a little further away. His back was turned away from me. Trying to prevent me from hearing?

As he finished the call and came back over, I smiled, trying to look nonchalant, but searching his face for signs of tension, or even secrecy.

'Everything OK?' I asked.

'Yes, yes. Just my mother, checking in.'

'What did she say?'

I could hear an accusatory tone creeping into my voice and instantly regretted it when he frowned at me.

'Just the usual,' he said lightly, sitting back down and looking away across the park, clearly not about to elaborate further.

I turned back to the sun, feeling a chill in spite of its heat that had nothing to do with the weather. He ran a hand lightly up my leg, but for once I didn't respond, even as I questioned myself. Had I heard him right, or was I hearing things to fit my own paranoia? And so what if he had mentioned her? There was no need to read anything into it.

But truth be told, although I couldn't bring myself to discuss it with Alex, his marital status and the things he had confided in me continued to play on my mind, in spite of the growing love between us . . . or perhaps because of. I constantly wondered if he ever compared me to his ex-wife, and although I tried to tell myself I was giving him something she clearly hadn't – submission – my jealousy remained. The thought of his previous subs bothered me less, for he had admitted they were just sex. But by having a relationship with him, I felt as though I were setting myself up for direct comparison with his ex – and no doubt, to my mind, coming up short. After all, I knew little about her; other than the fact that she was both wealthier and apparently far more sexually accomplished than I could ever hope to be.

I knew Alex would be horrified at the thoughts that gripped me at times, and for the most part I was deliriously in love, but every so often I was seized with an insecurity that left me reeling. I tried my best to separate past from present, but it preyed on my mind. As we explored in the bedroom, even Alex's prowess gave me pause for thought. He had learned all this with her, for her. She had initiated him. My innocence felt like a battle I had already lost, as much as Alex professed to love it, my inexperience a millstone around my neck. It led me to push myself further with him in the bedroom, trying to be everything he needed – while also pursuing my own desperate need for the sweet release our games brought me. For in that place, at his mercy, there was no room for worries or conflicting emotions, only the pleasure my surrender to him gave.

Only sometimes, afterwards, did I wonder just how much further it was possible to go, and if there would ever be any coming back from this. Or would I be for ever changed?

A few weeks later I was back in the playroom, again spread-eagled on the bed by the restraints, but this time face down. Alex knelt over me, massaging warm oil into my thighs and buttocks, each stroke of his hands inching closer and closer to the slit between my legs. He had placed the glass plug we had bought and a small, curved vibrator of my own next to my head where I could see them and thrill myself imagining the different scenarios he might be planning with them.

He had forbidden me to speak and so I lay still, enjoying the movement of his strong hands on my muscles, which ached from a long week at work in which I hadn't seemed to have a chance to sit down. Every so often he gave me a sharp slap across my cheeks, shocking me out of my comfort. The warm oil trickled down the crack of my ass and down between my parted legs, mingling with my own moisture. Alex ran a finger from back to front, circled my clit and came back up to my ass. His finger slipped inside me easily with all the oil, and he added another, turning them slightly inside me. I tipped my ass to him and moaned, and he spanked me.

'Be quiet. I don't want to hear a sound from you. If you make a noise, I'll take it as an indication you want to safe word, and I'll stop.'

I bit the bedding in frustration. I was as vocal as I had ever been with Alex and he usually encouraged me to scream and moan; now, once again, he switched the rules of the game. I buried my face in the bed and bit my lip as he lowered his head and I felt the tip of his tongue flickering around my asshole where his fingers entered me. It was an intrusive, almost unbearably intimate gesture – and that of course only made it all the more arousing. I ground my hips into the bed in an attempt to relieve the slow burn of my pussy, and he added another finger to my stretched ass, turning by small degrees as he slid them in and out. My body clenched around his fingers and he slowed his movements but didn't stop, relentlessly sliding deeper in and out of me. I felt my sex contract and widen, and as he removed his fingers I hoped he was turning his attention there, but instead he reached for the glass plug.

He slid it up and down between my legs, coating it with the oil. It was cold at first but quickly warmed to my body temperature, and he probed my ass with it before slipping the tip of it inside me. Using the same movements he had with his fingers he carefully fed the plug into me, twisting it carefully as it got wider and wider. It was a strange sensation; it felt wrong, forbidden, which to my chagrin only made me want it all the more. I felt full, the plug inside me heavy, causing a throbbing in my whole lower body. I wanted more, was aching for him to touch me again. I pulled against the restraints, unable even to put my hand in my mouth to stifle the cries I was desperate to utter. Keeping silent, along with the pressure of the plug, was building up the tension in my body like a pressure cooker. I squirmed desperately, to be rewarded with another slap across my cheeks and a sharp pull of my hair.

'Stay still. I'm going to fuck you now, while your arse is filled.'

He slid inside with no need for preparation; I was slick from the oil and my own arousal and I accepted him greedily even while fighting to hold myself still and quiet. He began to thrust into me with one hand pressing into the small of my back and the other buried in my hair, tugging on it now and then in a way that created a tingling all over my scalp. The feeling of being totally filled up and stretched by both his cock and the toy overwhelmed me and I opened my mouth in a silent scream into the duvet. I was close to orgasm and could feel myself tightening around him when he slowed down and then stopped, sliding himself out of me and removing the plug, turning it so it slipped out of me easily. I raised my head and tried to look back at him in mute appeal.

I wasn't disappointed; he replaced the plug with his cock, sliding deep into my now-ready ass. I bucked at the feel of him. He paused, stroking the small of my back, and then eased the full length of himself inside me, and I felt myself tighten around him. I lay still as he thrust slowly, acutely aware of the tiniest motion. It was almost unbearably intimate. As I gradually relaxed he increased his rhythm, then paused, reaching one hand back and picking up the vibrator. I gasped as I realised what he was doing, then quickly buried my head in the bed before he could scold me. I didn't want him to stop – God, no – and I knew if I disobeyed him he would do just that, making me beg for my own release. I squirmed again against the ties as, with his other hand, he slid the vibe into my soaking pussy, angling it towards my belly so that the curved tip pressed against that sensitive spot that had me gushing for him before. It must have been uncomfortable for him, having to lean down to manipulate the toy as he thrust into me, and I hoped he would untie my hands so I could take over, but of course he offered no such release, carrying on his relentless, ruthless penetration of both of my openings, causing everything in me to tighten and throb until my lower body was a pool of liquid heat, melting under him, my upper body taut as I pulled against the ties.

He built up his rhythm. My ass was fully open to him now and he picked up speed and depth, pounding into me, building up that delicious pressure inside me. He reached up and around my head, pushing two fingers into my mouth as he steadied himself on his elbow, and dipping them in and out of my throat as if he were playing with more intimate parts. It was such a simple yet shocking gesture; it tipped me totally over the edge until I was bucking my body against him, the bed, and the restraints. In that moment, he owned me, and I loved being his.

'Good girl,' he groaned, sounding close to the edge

himself. 'My dirty little fuckslut, look at you, with all three of your holes filled.'

His crude words sent me spinning into orgasm. I sucked hard on his fingers to keep from screaming as I climaxed, the added extra of the toy intensifying and prolonging my pleasure as wave after wave crashed over my body. He bellowed like an animal as he pounded into me, reaching his own climax and then collapsing on top of my back, burying his face in my neck and hair, panting and kissing the side of my face with fevered lips. We were both soaked with sweat and oil and my juices.

'I love you,' he moaned, as if in pain, and I chuckled.

'I would say it back, but you told me not to speak, Sir,' I said cheekily, and he laughed into my neck, too spent even to spank me.

And so there was another line crossed, and yet more territory that he had conquered.

Journal extract

It's been such a good week! Alex is still amazing. We just seem to fit so well – not just in bed, but in every way.

I introduced Alex to Kim last night. I'm not sure if they were too keen on each other, to be honest, but then she's always like that with my boyfriends. We're doing the 'family thing' this week. His sister, Maria. My mum. Now that should be a barrel of laughs – not.

I'm curious to see what Maria is like, though, and to see a different side of Alex.

I need to know more about who he is in areas other than the bedroom . . .

Chapter Sixteen

'You must be Kelly. Finally!'

I liked Maria as soon as she flung open the door with what I soon learned was characteristic flair. Knowing she was a teacher, and what with Alex's sometimes stern persona, I had expected a very different woman to the chic and vivacious girl who opened the door and threw her arms around Alex, and then me, before ushering us in with a wide grin. She was beautiful, of course; darker than Alex, showing her Cypriot roots, and only a year older than me, with an infectious energy that made you smile just being near her.

'Ah, Alex, she's gorgeous,' she enthused, linking her arm with mine and leading me into the front room, which was beautifully decorated but a total shambles.

Two dark, sticky children, both under four, played with different coloured pieces of dough on an expensive-looking cream rug that I doubted would remain cream for long. Such a contrast to Alex's show home. I raised an amused eyebrow as the children rushed over to him with cries of 'Uncle Alex!' and 'Have you brought sweets?'

Watching him swing them around, I did that swooning thing women do when they see their man with children, and wondered what our own would look like.

Returning to reality with a wry smile, I headed into the kitchen to help Maria with drinks before Alex spotted my dreamy expression. She chattered away nineteen to the dozen, firing questions at me but not giving me time to answer.

'I'm sorry, you'll get used to me,' she said. 'It's just so nice to see Alex happy; he's done nothing but talk about you.'

'Really?'

I was surprised, not having thought he was the confiding type. He wasn't one to go into much detail about his family, and I hadn't realised how close he obviously was to his sister. She went on, telling me more about him in five minutes than he had told me in months.

'Alex is like our pops, or tries to be. Very alpha-male, very traditional. He was such a high achiever at school – the best at sports, the head prefect, everything. He'll take over the family business when Pops retires, just because it's expected of him. And he could have been a footballer, you know; he had trials back home. But Pops was having none of it. They've been butting heads for years, but Alex is our dad through and through. I hope you don't let him boss you around?'

I concealed a smirk at that. There were some things that I was betting she didn't know about her brother.

'Was your father strict with you, being a girl?' I asked, noticing a tattoo on her wrist peeking out from under her sleeve. Something else we had in common.

'Oh, yes. Catholic schools, the lot. But I was always the wild child of the family. I escaped over here after Alex as quick as I could. It's better now that I'm married and teaching; I think my parents expected me to run off with the circus or something.'

I laughed. I felt relaxed and at home, and as if I knew Alex a lot better; another layer had been peeled away. By the time he came into the kitchen, a child on his shoulders, I was comparing tattoos with Maria. Alex groaned in mock horror.

'What are those silly ladies doing, Petey?' he addressed his nephew. 'Shall we leave them to it and go and play in the garden?'

'Yay, Uncle Alex do horsey!' the child whooped, bouncing about on his shoulders.

I watched in wonder as Alex proceeded to trot round the garden with him.

'He'll make a wonderful father,' Maria observed, looking at me slyly under her long lashes.

'Mmm,' I responded nonchalantly, desperately searching for a way to change the subject, but Maria did it for me.

'I'm so glad he got away from that cow Frances, but since they separated he's not seemed interested in meeting anyone else. You'll do him the world of good.'

'What was she like?' I asked, wondering how much Maria knew.

I was pretty sure Alex wouldn't discuss his sexual proclivities with his little sister; she was obviously unaware of the 'flings' he had had since his marriage had ended, though given the nature of them I reasoned that was hardly surprising.

'Beautiful, but a total bitch. Always looked down on me, too. I was still a wild teenager when they first got together; I don't think she ever forgave me for telling Alex I thought she was a stuck-up cow. Mama and Pops loved her, though; she still phones them sometimes. But don't worry: they'll love you, when Alex takes you over.'

Oh, God. I was suddenly glad his parents lived in Cyprus. With any luck Frances would be out of the picture by the time I met them.

'I'm sure she only keeps in touch with them to annoy Alex. It's been nearly two years now, but she still hasn't got over him leaving her. Good riddance, I say.'

Maria motioned me back into the front room and I followed her, feeling a sudden chill. Her little girl, now covered in green playdough, looked up and gave me a toothy grin.

'Uncle Alex in love,' she stated.

Maria beamed, picking her up.

'That's right, darling. He certainly is.'

I basked in her approval.

From the warm loving bubble of Maria's home to my mother's . . . This was the part I was not looking forward to. With my stepfather away on a fishing trip, there wasn't even his presence to diffuse the tension. She opened the door; as usual looking at me as if the cat had brought me in on her paws, then looked at Alex. And she blushed. She actually blushed.

'So you're Alex? So nice to meet you at last,' she simpered.

I gazed at her, open-mouthed. I spent the next hour

in mostly silent bemusement as my mother fawned over Alex, who went into perfect-gentleman mode, complimenting her décor and garden and even her hair. I was still dazed when we left, and she leaned over to me for a tentative hug.

'Try and hang on to this one, for God's sake,' she murmured.

I smiled tightly.

As soon I sat down in the car I let out a sigh I hadn't even realised I'd been holding. Alex reached over and began kneading at my shoulders.

'That wasn't so bad, was it? She reminds me of my father, you know; doesn't know how to show her feelings except by criticising.'

'She loved you,' I sniped.

He smiled, squeezing the back of my neck in firm circles until I relaxed further. He leaned over and kissed me on the forehead, a gesture that touched me even as he slipped a hand up my sedate knee-length skirt and gently pinched my clit. I yelped in surprise, and he winked at me.

'Let's get you back and see what we can do with the rest of that tension, shall we?'

'Sounds fantastic.'

Once the 'family thing' had been done, it felt more official. We spent more time with Maria and her husband, and even with my parents, the presence of Alex making things less strained between my mother and myself. My stepdad, never one to say much, nodded at me after the first time they had met: 'He seems all right.'

Having just spent the night tied to Alex's bed while he paddled me, I could only grin in agreement.

The sex continued to be as intense as ever, and I fell deeper in love with each encounter. Being with Alex had cast a glow over all areas of my life. I was more creative at work, more energetic at the gym and more relaxed with my friends.

'You're blossoming,' Kim remarked.

The only blip came when Alex went to Cyprus for another two weeks during the summer holidays. I had pretty much been expecting an invitation, so I pouted like a schoolgirl when none was forthcoming. He tried to reassure me, spending the night at mine before he left for the airport and holding me until it was light.

'I just want to wait until the divorce is through before I introduce you to them. My parents are very traditional. We're talking a matter of weeks before the decree absolute arrives,' he told me, stroking my hair.

I didn't voice my fears, not wanting to reveal my petty jealousies to him, but what were the chances she would phone while he was there? I tried to shake the thought from my mind; he had left her, he was hardly pining for her, but nevertheless she felt like a threat. And if his parents were so upset about the divorce, would they ever accept me? I tried to give myself a strict talking-to. I had to stop trying to run before we were even walking; it was still a relatively new relationship, after all. I should be enjoying each moment, not worrying about the future or his past. BDSM should have taught me that, if nothing else; it was all about the moment.

But the two weeks were intolerably long, even though

we spoke every day on the phone. I felt lost, unable even to remember what I used to do with myself before Alex.

'You need to get a grip,' Kim said in her straight-to-the-point way.

When he returned, I threw myself into his arms and he picked me up so I could wrap my legs around his waist.

'I've missed you,' he said into my mouth as he kissed me, hands squeezing my ass where he held me up. 'I'm not going over again until I can take you with me.'

'I'm not letting you go without me,' I said back, only half-joking. He set me down and stared at me in mock horror.

'Two weeks away and you think you're the boss. Oh dear.' He smiled wickedly, slapping me gently on the side of the face and then kissing me swiftly in the same spot as if to counteract it. 'You had better get in that bedroom.'

My face split into a wide grin.

'Oh, yes, Sir.'

Journal extract

It's a bank holiday, so I'm going to spend a long weekend at Alex's. Just me and him. He wants to 'explore things further', apparently. I'm not sure how much further there is. I'm excited – but also more than a little scared.

He said he wants to explore my submissiveness. To make me fully give myself to him. I thought I already had . . . especially after I was so bereft when he went away earlier in the holidays. Yet Alex says that he can still sense me hesitating at times. He says I need to completely surrender.

But I don't really know what that means – or how I'll know when I have.

I still can't believe how much I've changed since I met him. I feel softer; it's like I'm looking at the world through rose-tinted glasses. I didn't even realise how wound up I usually am; it's like he's released years of tension.

I'm excited to see what he's got in store for me this weekend. I'd better go and pack my bag. I'm taking that new underwear he bought me, but I bet I won't be wearing it for long . . .

Chapter Seventeen

'The lingerie looks beautiful on you,' Alex said, as he admired his new purchase: red and black lace, with a balconette bra that made my breasts look higher and fuller on my chest, and cute matching French knickers cut just right to frame my ass.

I have a big butt for such a small girl, but Alex's obvious appreciation of my curves had enhanced my body image and I was beginning to love dressing up for him. He had a brilliant eye for colours and shapes, and though I hadn't thought the lingerie set particularly exciting when he first picked it, I had to admit his choice was perfect. I did a little twirl for him, admiring myself in the full-length mirror in his bedroom.

'Leave it on for dinner,' he commanded, running a fingertip across my cleavage, leaving a trail of goosebumps across my skin. His touch still thrilled me as much as it had in the beginning, if not more so.

Sitting at dinner in my underwear, with Alex still in his work suit, I felt sexy, especially as his eyes drank me in with appreciation. Alex had always had a way of making me feel beautiful, and it wasn't just about compliments or lingering looks; even over his knee being spanked, or on my own knees calling him 'Sir' and answering to 'slut', I never felt anything less than adored. It was a heady, intoxicating feeling. I sipped my wine demurely, legs elegantly crossed, playing the lady in my lacy French underwear. He set a plate of steaming food down in front of me: spiced lamb with couscous and roasted Mediterranean vegetables, typical Alex food. It was more than I wanted, but it made me smile; I knew that if he was attempting to 'feed me up' then he was planning on putting me through my paces over the weekend.

'Eat,' he ordered.

He was taciturn and unsmiling, a cue that I knew meant he was in dom mode, and so I ate obediently, keeping my eyes down. Inside, I was buzzing with anticipation, a hundred different scenarios running through my head.

He had put some music on: edgy rock ballads that I loved but didn't think would be to Alex's taste. My taste in music ran from Kylie to Coheed and Cambria whereas Alex was more of a blues and jazz guy. I was tapping my foot to the beat as I pushed my plate away. It was still half full and he glowered at me, but relented, for which I breathed a sigh of relief. The only gripe I had with him was his annoying monitoring of my diet. A three-meals-a-day guy, he could never get his head around my haphazard approach to feeding myself. But he had more than a good meal on the agenda tonight. He came round behind me, pulling a black silk tie from his pocket. I grinned, and then resumed my demure expression. Things were about to get interesting. Oh, goody.

He tied the silk around my eyes, and then pulled my arms back behind my chair before tying my wrists with something thinner and more knotted, but still soft. He pulled my chair so I was facing out towards him and I heard his footsteps retreat into the kitchen. As I sat and waited for his next move I could already feel the heat rising in me and my breath becoming shorter.

Subspace was beckoning. I let it happen. That space Anna had talked about, that place where all that exists is you, your dominant and the sensations, was becoming easier and easier for me to access; just a touch or a certain look from Alex now were enough for me to yield. It had been a natural process, there had been no overt 'training' as such on his part, and if it was his intention this weekend to push me even further into that zone I doubted I would ever come back. I was a raw nerve, quivering with desire by the time I heard him approach me again. He ran something cold across my stomach, making me jump and bringing me back to reality.

'Open your mouth.'

I paused, unsure what object he was holding, but obeyed as he pushed something cold and hard to my lips. I was relieved as I bit down. Strawberry. I chewed it slowly, enjoying the taste, which was extra-sweet from having been chilled.

'Good girl. And again. Suck it this time.'

This one was covered in dark chocolate, and I sucked it vigorously. I could get used to this. After a few more, he ordered me to stand up, helping me lift my bound hands over the chair, and guided me upstairs. Clumsy as ever, walking around blindfolded is definitely not my strong point and he had to steady me a few times before he managed to lead me safely into the bedroom. He untied my hands but kept the blindfold on, pushing me back on to the bed. As far as I could tell we were in his room rather than the playroom, so I wondered what he had planned. He lifted my head, pushing a wine glass to my lips. It was Champagne, and when I finished drinking he tipped some of it across my stomach. He licked across my skin, then poured some more across my cleavage, and then, parting my legs, across my inner thighs.

'You'll ruin the underwear,' I protested weakly, as he lapped at the sensitive spots high up on my inner thigh, and I felt his hot breath on me through the knickers.

He moved up, burying his face in my cleavage as he lapped up the rest of the Champagne. Then he kissed me, passing the last of the liquid into my mouth. It fizzed briefly on my tongue until he kissed me more deeply, invading my mouth, and I responded with hunger, my hands going up to his back to trace over the strong muscles that rippled beneath his shoulders. He pulled away, panting, and breathed deeply – regaining his control, I knew. When I felt him get up I went to sit up with him, but he pushed me back down.

'Stay still, baby. I haven't finished playing with you.'

I lay back and surrendered to him. I was enjoying this soft play, especially as I was pretty sure it was a prelude to harder games, and I felt decadent and pampered in my expensive underwear and with my skin still sticky from the Champagne. Something touched me. It tickled across my stomach and my cleavage and down again to the band of my knickers. It was light and soft, raising goose pimples across me. It took me a few moments to realise it was a feather. He leaned over me and tugged at my pants with his mouth. I lifted my hips so they could slide down and went to help with my hands, but he pushed me away.

'Put your hands over your head and keep them there, baby, understand?'

'Yes, Sir.'

The lace slid down my thighs and over my feet, which he took in his mouth and kissed, swirling his tongue around the arches and sucking on my toes like he would on my nipples. It was incredibly arousing, and I sighed with pleasure as he began to kiss his way back up my leg. He broke off just as he reached the melting heat of my pussy, replacing his mouth with the feather, stroking it around the very tops of my thighs, my outer lips and up over my pubic bone. He moved it so slowly that it was a sweet torture, and I bit my lip with frustration and opened my legs wider. He stroked the tip of the feather over my clit, making me gasp. If he kept it up, I felt sure I could come just from this.

But the feather went away, to be replaced by something thick and soft. Fur. He trailed it across my throat, down over my body and all the way down my legs and up in between them, up and over my pussy and flicking across my hips. It was luxuriously soft on my skin, a different sensation again from the feather, and I was unprepared for him to suddenly grab my hips and roll me on to my front, giving me a sharp slap across the cheeks of my ass.

'Your arse is so spankable,' he growled, kneading the flesh where he had just slapped.

Then I felt the fur again, running all over my back and bottom, teasing the back of my thighs and nudging them apart. He drew it very slowly up in between my legs and the cleft between my cheeks, across my back and shoulders, then back down, and then up again, over and over, until my whole body was sensitised. I was by now craving a harder touch, tipping my ass up to him in a silent request. He complied, spanking me hard a few times in swift succession, and I moaned aloud. Yes, that was what I wanted, almost needed. But it was over too soon. He rolled me over and pulled off the blindfold, kissing me and then sitting back on his haunches. He looked amused, and I frowned at him, confused.

'You are going to suck my cock now, and make me come down that lovely little throat of yours. And then, we sleep.'

'Sleep?' I think my mouth must have dropped open with shock.

Alex nodded.

'You will have to earn your orgasm this weekend, by showing me total surrender. I'm looking forward to it.'

I gaped at him. I knew what he was doing: orgasm denial. Knowing Alex, he would drag this out as long as he possibly could, until I was a whimpering mess. My body ached in protest, but I didn't utter a word, simply bent down to free his cock and took him in my mouth. He stroked my hair tenderly.

'Good girl.'

True to his word, after he had come in thick streams that I drank down greedily, he threw the quilt back and motioned for us to get into bed, spooning me as he usually did, a leg thrown over my hip. He kissed the back of my neck, whispering, 'Don't let me feel you trying to touch yourself, or I will have to put you in the cuffs.'

'Yes, Sir,' I said, more grumpy than submissive.

He chuckled and then yawned. I was sure it was for effect.

'Night, baby.'

I didn't reply.

I woke the next morning after a broken sleep, filled with erotic dreams in which Alex had tied me to the cross and stroked me with the fur while a room full of people looked on. He stood over me, his hair awry from sleep but looking otherwise fresh, with a plate of bacon and eggs and a glass of orange juice.

'Babe, that smells lovely, but you know I can't eat first thing in the morning.' I've never been able to eat breakfast.

'Then you had better start. Sit up.'

He placed the tray on my lap, and my stomach growled loudly. Obviously I was hungrier than I thought, and I tucked in.

'I'll turn the shower on. Come in to me when you're done.'

He dropped a kiss on my forehead. I ate quickly, gulping down my orange juice, and went to join him, discarding my bra, which was all I had on from the night before.

He was already in the shower and I took a few moments to admire him before stepping in, noting the curve of his muscled thighs and buttocks and the broadness of his back. I still sometimes wanted to pinch myself; I was so amazed he was mine. Or, in keeping with the theme of the weekend, that I was his. I stepped in behind him, sliding the glass door closed and putting my arms round him to knead his chest from behind. He turned to me, his hair dark and close to his face with the water, which made his green eyes all the more piercing. I moved in for a kiss but he edged himself around behind me, pushed me up to the tiles and used a knee to part my legs.

'I'm going to wash you,' he said as he reached for the soap.

Lathering it up in his hands he kneaded my buttocks and thighs in the same infuriating moves he had used the night before, always just grazing my pussy without ever fully touching me. He moved his hands round, soaping up my breasts and fondling them with practised ease, before reaching for the shower head and running the hot water down my back and legs. He moved it in circles as he moved up the inside of my thighs, the water drumming against my skin. I parted my legs as he moved the shower head between them and jumped when a jet of water touched my clit. He pulled away slightly to decrease the intensity but kept it there, running the water directly over the tip, making me gasp. He reached around to fondle my breasts with his other hand, tweaking my nipples and pinching them in turn.

'Harder,' I begged, as he rolled a nipple between thumb and forefinger, waves of pleasure rolling through me, bringing me towards a ready climax I knew he wouldn't allow me to have.

On cue, he moved the shower head just as I felt the familiar tightening low in my body that heralded an intense orgasm. I groaned in frustration, begging him even though I knew it would be futile. After his statement the previous evening, I knew he wouldn't let me take my pleasure so readily. Perhaps this was what he meant by 'total surrender': giving him control over even the moment of release. Placing my pleasure thoroughly in his hands. The contractions subsided, leaving my body tight with frustration. Within minutes the shower head was back, along with his knuckles, rubbing against me. I was amazed by how quickly the sensations began to build again, even more intense, and the pangs of frustration when he pulled the shower away again were actually painful, my clit uncomfortably sensitive. I turned round as he showered the soap from my breasts, pleading with my eyes. I couldn't take a whole weekend of this. I was on the edge already.

He was erect, obviously as turned on as I was, his cheeks flushed from more than the heat. I wanted to reach for him, to feel his wet skin on mine, but he turned off the shower and stepped out, passing me a towel. He wrapped it around me, staring into my face. His eyes had that dark, narrowed look that I recognised as his dominant gaze, almost predatory with desire, and I wanted to grab him, take him into me and ride him until I was sated. It was a thought totally at odds with the submissive role I was playing and I dropped my eyes. He gripped my chin, lifting my face back up to his.

'I love that look on your face. Almost pissed off, yet you can't hide how much you want me.'

He was right: I never could hide it; my lust would be written plain across my face. I got out of the shower and rubbed myself dry, and had to wince when the towel brushed against my pussy, the denying of my orgasm having left me too sensitive to touch.

'I need to go to the study and do some work,' Alex said as he dressed. 'Come down to me when you're done. I want you undressed and wearing nothing but your collar.'

I swallowed.

'Yes, Sir.'

I took my time getting dry, moisturising myself thoroughly with a musky lotion I knew he loved the smell of, blow-drying my hair into loose curls and applying just a touch of make-up, then fastening the collar around my neck. I added a pair of spike heels I had borrowed from Kim; they had delicate chains running around the ankles, which added, I thought, a very appropriate touch.

I entered his study with what I hoped was an alluring walk, my eyes down. He was sitting at his desk, tapping away at his keyboard, and didn't even look up. Deliberately, I guessed.

'Kneel over there in the corner' – he tipped his head to indicate the far corner by the window, only just out of sight of people walking past – 'and put your hands on your thighs.'

I went to do as I was told, kneeling on the plush carpet, fighting the urge to cover myself as I walked past the window. He looked over, appraising me.

'Open your legs some more, and keep your eyes down.'

So there I knelt, my hands on my legs, looking at the floor, while Alex typed away. When he began making a few work calls, I looked up in horror, and then lowered my eyes again at his frown. He was brief and brisk on the phone, his tone of course betraying nothing about the fact that there was a naked, collared woman kneeling just a few feet away. He replaced the handset and went back to his

188

computer, not looking at me once. My legs were restless, and I shifted position. Alex glowered at me.

'I don't want you to move. You will stay still until I tell you otherwise.'

I nodded, watching from under my eyelashes as he opened a drawer and took out a long, thin cane. He laid it on the desk in front of him.

'I will count every time I see you move; and for each count you get a slap with this, as well as more time in that corner, so I suggest you behave.'

I sighed inwardly. It was going to be a long morning if that was the case; the urge to fidget was growing stronger by the minute, no doubt especially because I had been told not to.

The longer I knelt there, the more I began to understand what he had meant by 'total surrender'. Not just to his demands or even to my own inner desires, but mentally and emotionally, too. Time stretched and wore thin as I tried to relax and concentrate on my breathing and my body, giving in to the moment. Much like meditation, I thought, until the thought itself interrupted any meditative state of mind. Every time I sneaked a glance at the clock I was amazed to see how slowly the hands were moving. I wondered if it was his plan to keep me there until I had to move and disobey, so that he had an excuse to punish me. I bit my lip in anticipation, not wanting to defy him, yet eager to see how he would punish me if I did. I knelt there for no more than half an hour, but it was easily the longest half-hour I had ever experienced. I let out a long breath of relief when he ordered me to stand, and got to my feet slowly, rubbing my legs.

'Feel better?'

'Yes, thank you, Sir.'

'You did very well,' he said warmly. 'I'm quite disappointed, you hardly moved at all. Perhaps I should just cane you anyway?'

I smiled.

'Perhaps you should, Sir,' I said, walking towards him as he patted his knee, the thought of anyone peeking in as I passed the window now adding a frisson of excitement.

I realised I wanted to go over his knee. He hadn't spanked me in this position since that first time, and I was eager to recreate the moment.

I quickly discovered, however, that being spanked with a cane is very different from a hand, and the first blow stung sharply. Upended, my head hanging down his legs and my palms flat on the floor, I flinched away from the cane as he brought it down again. Sensing my discomfort, he made the next few blows less harsh, before stopping to give my injured buttocks a soothing rub. He ran his knuckles across my pussy lips where they peeked between my cheeks and my body responded with a rush of heat. He pushed his thumb inside me, then withdrew it, and I heard him suck it.

'You taste gorgeous,' he said, and I murmured a thank you, flinching when he brought the cane down again.

'You really are a naughty slut, aren't you?' he said, almost as if talking to himself.

The moan I gave as he caressed me was answer enough. He hit me again, and I felt myself falling into that expansive space I was beginning to crave. He lifted me up and turned me round, my sore cheeks resting against the edge of his desk, and then knelt down and buried his face in me. I ground my hips at him, leaning back on my hands, loving the change in position; him on his knees for me, for once. He licked and sucked at me until I was gripping the sides of the desk, my legs trembling with a will of their own.

And then he took the power back. Moving away just at that crucial moment, leaving me feeling as if my body was throbbing with need. The frustration was intense, a sensation I'd never experienced before, and I gave an animal groan, glaring at him. I pressed my own hand against my tortured pussy, more to soothe than to please. Of course he moved it, raising it to his mouth and sucking my fingers, damp from just that brief touch. He kissed me, and I could taste my own musky scent on his lips. I pushed myself against him wantonly, feeling his erection through his trousers as he nibbled at my ear.

'You can stop this, honey. Just safe word and I'll let you come. We can spend the rest of the weekend visiting garden centres, or something equally dull.'

I barked a laugh, shaking my head even as my body raged in protest. This had become a challenge now, a subtle power game involving a certain kind of control on both our parts. I realised that perhaps he was right, there was just a tiny part of me still holding back, and I suddenly wanted to cling on to it with both hands. For if I gave him everything, what would be left?

We had a late lunch, with me naked at the table, pressing my thighs together to ease the unsatisfied ache. He didn't touch me again all afternoon. We lay on the couch watching films, with me at his feet while he stroked my hair. I drifted off at some point, tired from sheer restlessness. When I woke, it was dusk, and Alex was nowhere to be seen. The TV was off and the fire flickering away and I was tempted to stay put, but curiosity got the better of me and I wandered upstairs. Alex looked up as I entered the playroom and smiled. He had the black rope he had bought from the sex shop weeks ago in his hands.

'Sorry, I fell asleep.'

'Not at all,' he said. 'It can take it out of you, I know. How is your butt? The cane can be harsh.'

I rubbed my ass, wincing and smiling at the same time.

'Sore,' I admitted.

'How sore? Feel up to a little light bondage?'

He held up the ropes. My heart instantly began to beat faster.

'What did you have in mind, Sir?' I quipped, walking towards him.

He stood, holding the ropes up to my naked body, assessing them again.

'Ever heard of *Kinbaku*?' he asked, by way of explanation.

I shook my head at the exotic-sounding word.

'It's a form of bondage from Japan, using ropes. It involves some very intricate patterns; it's an art form, in fact. Something I thought you might appreciate, given your love of body art.'

'OK,' I shrugged, thinking it didn't sound particularly sexy, but then neither, on paper, did rabbit fur and nipple clamps.

Alex stepped behind me.

'Put your hands behind your back, as if you're holding the opposite elbows. To make a square,' he ordered.

I put my arms into the strange position, similar to one I had seen at the yoga class Kim and I had sporadically attended. It caused a slight tightness in my upper arms, but it wasn't too uncomfortable. Still, that would depend on how long he expected me to hold it. Any more kneeling in corners and I was going to explode.

'This is a traditional box tie. The correct term is *ushiro takatekote*, and it's the basic position. It's quite comfortable; you'll be able to hold it for a while.'

I groaned audibly, and he gave my bottom a playful swat.

'Relax, I won't keep you trussed up any longer than you can handle. Turn round; let me do your breasts.'

My breasts? I turned round as directed, watching with interest now as he looped another length of rope around me, underneath my breasts and then around them, so they were pressed from all angles, causing them to pop out, my nipples and the fleshiest parts protruding from between the ropes. He then wound the ropes around the tops of my arms and shoulders, constricting my arms further. By the time he had finished, it looked as if I was wearing a very intricate bra, the position of my arms and the ropes around my chest pushing my breasts towards him like an offering. He flicked my engorged nipples, bending down to take one in his mouth, sucking it until it stuck right out, then moving to the other. Admiring his handiwork, he pinched them both roughly. It sent a shiver right through my body, made all the more intense by my inability to move my upper torso.

He picked up another rope.

'For your crotch,' he explained when I looked at him questioningly, and I swallowed.

'Won't it hurt?'

'Not when it's done properly. Though I intend to cause a little friction . . .' He winked at me.

He wound the rope around my waist and down, positioning it over the slit between my outer lips. He tugged it, judging its tightness, and then tied a knot. When he wound it underneath me and tied it to the ropes behind my back, I realised he had positioned the knot so that it sat right on my clitoris. He pulled lightly on the rope and the knot rubbed maddeningly on my clit. Thankfully, after the food and sleep, the sensitivity had waned, but the way my body was responding I knew it wouldn't be long before I was once again at fever pitch.

I stood very, very still indeed as he reached for the nipple clamps, part of me longing to feel the pinch of them while another wondered if I could take the extra stimulation. He fastened them carefully, mindful of the way my pressed, pushed-out breasts were already swollen and aching. He stepped back, looking me over. I felt a little silly, and far more exposed than I had walking around naked all day, but when he turned me round to see myself in the mirror I gasped in delight.

'You look beautiful like this.'

I had to agree. The fine black ropes framed and outlined every curve of my body, my breasts looked bigger and perkier and inviting even to my own eyes, the crotch rope disappearing between my thighs, offering a sinful line of sight. The black ropes stood out in stark contrast against my white skin, emphasising the dark fall of my hair and the collar around my neck. My tattoos, a tumble of vines over one shoulder and again down the opposite thigh, only added to the visual. The overall impression was erotic yet ethereally stunning. I felt as though I were looking at someone else, a goddess from some secret place.

Alex ran his hands over me and I watched as he fondled my breasts and pulled at the clamps, and tugged on the rope at my clit with short, insistent strokes. I saw my cheeks flush in the mirror, my pupils so dilated with desire my eyes were almost black. Alex bit the sensitive spot on my neck, the dip where it met my shoulder, and I shuddered.

'It looks amazing,' I whispered.

'You are amazing. I have to photograph you like this one day. Can you walk comfortably?'

I took a few steps. The rope pulled at my crotch in maddening tugs, but I could move. I nodded.

'Good. Go into the playroom and kneel down. Put your forehead to the floor.'

The short walk to the playroom was excruciating, every step causing the soft ropes to move against my pussy, and I could feel an insistent throbbing that only grew stronger as I knelt down, the position pulling the rope that bit tighter and pulling back on my breasts, too, so that my nipples, almost forgotten amid the all-consuming burn at the centre of my pussy, ached in unison. He had to let me come soon, surely; I was so close now I thought the slightest touch would send me off. If he continued to hold out on me . . . Well, let's just say garden centres were looking tempting.

I heard him behind me, felt him kneel down and run a hand over my exposed bum and felt that he was naked. He pushed his erection against me, reaching around to tug on the clamps.

'Do you want me to fuck you?'

'Yes, Sir.'

'But can you stop yourself from coming? If you let yourself come, I shall have to punish you some more.'

I bit my lip.

'I'll try, Sir,' I ground out, torn between allowing him to continue to torment me and surrendering to the need in me.

He slipped off the clamps, kneading my breasts as my nipples ached unbearably, and loosened the rope around my waist to give himself access to me, but still keep a slight pressure. He slid into me easily, holding my bound arms for leverage. Tied up and bent over, I was fully exposed to him, fully on display.

'You're so wet,' he murmured, finding his rhythm and moving in long, deep thrusts, pulling back on my arms, upping the stimulation around my breasts, each thrust sliding the rope, now slick with my arousal, back and forth against my clit.

Had I not been so wet it would have been uncomfortable. As it was, it felt delicious. My face was screwed up with tension as I desperately tried to hold off my orgasm, to halt the advance of the waves of pleasure rolling up and through my body. When his breathing grew faster and his movements more frantic, I lost any control I was still holding on to, my orgasm breaking over me in spite of my attempts to hold it back. It seemed to go on and on, wave after wave crashing over me, the contractions coming from deep in my belly, right from my centre. I felt I was melting into him, like liquid fire in his arms, only vaguely aware of his own bellowing as he climaxed inside me. I gave him everything, my back arching, head tipped back in total abandonment. I had a single stunning moment of perfect clarity – that this was it, this was what it was about – before I burst into tears. My screams turned to sobs as the orgasm subsided, the tears hot on my cheeks. Alex untied me with swift, deft hands, pulling me into his arms, his face horrified.

'Shit, are you OK?'

I smiled through my tears at him, unable to explain why I was crying. I was laughing and sobbing simultaneously.

'It's just the release, I think. I'm not sad,' was the best I could offer.

And I wasn't sad – far from it. I felt somehow cleansed, as if every bit of tension I had ever been holding had poured out of me. I snuggled into him as he pushed my hair, damp with sweat, away from my face.

'I couldn't hold back,' I apologised.

Alex gave a shaky laugh.

'Neither could I. I'm finding it increasingly difficult to keep in control with you. As much as I love you submitting to me, I'm no longer sure who's really in charge here.'

I pulled back, scanning his face. I didn't understand. I had just let go more thoroughly and completely than I had thought possible. Perhaps he had felt it, too.

'As your dominant, I should be able to keep a level of detachment, but . . .' – he paused here, as if choosing his words carefully – 'but it's becoming increasingly harder . . . the more I fall in love with you.'

'I'll be strapping you to crosses soon,' I said lightly, and then laughed at the look on his face. 'Or maybe not that soon.'

In all honesty I couldn't imagine us 'switching', the idea of stalking around with a whip in my hand having as little appeal to me as the idea of being submissive had for him. We fit the way we were.

'Have you not felt like that before?' I wanted to add '. . . with Frances', but held back. This wasn't the time. And for the first time I didn't care; she didn't matter.

He shook his head, looking at me seriously.

'No, I haven't. I feel like I'm losing myself in you. I was planning on keeping the orgasm denial going until tomorrow, but as soon as I was inside you, I lost all thought. It was remiss of me.'

'What's the thrill of being in control all the time, anyway?' I asked.

I genuinely didn't get it. The benefits for me were obvious, but for him, I couldn't see the allure. Whatever pleasure he took from seeing me surrender to him, from taking me to that place, was surely only second-hand.

'I'm not sure if it's a thrill as much as a compulsion,' he shrugged, 'but the edges are becoming very blurred with you.'

'Before you know it, we'll be having sex in the missionary position with the lights off on Saturday nights only.'

'You kinky bitch,' he murmured into my ear, and I howled with laughter, the ropes that were still trailing from my body shaking with me. I felt giddy, almost ecstatic.

He picked me up as if I weighed nothing, carrying me into the bedroom and laying me back on the bed. As he bent down and kissed me I felt a thrill of arousal and parted my legs beneath him without even being aware of my movements. He looked down at me quizzically, a smile tugging at the edges of his mouth.

'Have I not worn you out yet?'

In answer, I slid a hand down his torso to his cock. I would have thought his body would be spent for a while at least, yet I felt him stirring under my hand. I squeezed and he groaned, nibbling on my lip.

'Minx,' he whispered, slipping a hand between my legs. I was slick with his climax and mine, and his fingers slipped into me with ease.

Three fingers stroked my inner walls expertly as he rubbed the pad of his thumb over my clitoris. Already soaking and open for him, my body gave him little resistance as he added a fourth finger. I felt stretched, filled up, yet still pushed my hips upwards, silently asking for more.

'Are you sure?' he whispered again, and I nodded breathlessly, not really able to articulate exactly what it was I was asking for, but knowing that I wanted as much of him as I could take.

He removed his fingers for a moment, then slowly slipped them in again, holding his hand palm up, fingers and thumb pushed together in the middle. I raised myself on my elbows and watched as he slid them in to me, starting with his fingertips and then moving slowly in until his thumb tip and knuckles were at the entrance to my pussy. My juices glistened on his hand. I whimpered with a heady mixture of almost unbearable pressure and a deep ache of desire as he twisted his hand, slipping the widest part of it in. I moaned, a long-drawn-out sound, tipping my head back until my hair pooled on his sheets.

'Go on, baby,' I urged him, bucking my hips upward as I felt him ball his hand inside me.

He moved his hand in a slow rhythm inside me and I jerked my pelvis again, impatient. He stopped moving.

'I don't want to hurt you,' he said, caressing my thigh with his free hand, 'so I'm going to keep my hand still. You move, baby. Fuck my hand.'

There was no hesitation in me now at his commands. I tilted myself backwards and forwards, needing only tiny movements to feed my arousal, the pressure inside me was so intense. I moved quicker, my hips rising and falling, my hands clutching at my breasts and pulling at their stiff peaks that were still aching from the clamps. Alex grabbed my hair suddenly, yanking my head up so that I could see his fist inside of me.

'Look,' he growled, and at the sight of him buried in me up to the wrist I climaxed again, my whole body contracting.

It was almost painful, ripping through me, and when it was over I collapsed back on to the bed, my head whirling in shock. As my orgasm subsided I began to ache; his hand inside me was suddenly too much and I winced as he turned and uncurled it. There was a single moment of pressure that made me yelp and then his hand slid out of me in a rush of my own wetness.

Shaking and tired, I collapsed again on to the sheets, fighting an overwhelming urge to sleep. He curled in behind me, stroking my side and kissing my shoulder, murmuring sweet nothings. My eyes fluttered.

'Go to sleep,' he said, throwing a warm arm around me. I could feel his erection pushing into my back.

'But you're not done,' I protested.

I felt him shake his head behind me.

'Just go to sleep,' he ordered. 'I can wait.'

When I woke in the morning, yawning and stretching, I was immediately aware of a dull throb between my legs. The events of the night before came rushing back, and as I rolled over to see Alex awake and watching me, my cheeks flushed.

'I feel like I've lost my virginity all over again,' I confessed, pressing a hand to my pussy.

It wasn't entirely painful; the ache was similar to that of my buttocks the day after he had spanked or whipped me: it made you wince, but at the same time each sting brought a throb of remembered desire. The line between pleasure and pain really is a very fine one. I was glad Alex had some idea of what he was doing, or I think in the heat of the moment I could easily have pushed my body too far. Hence me being the bottom, and Alex the top.

He was caressing my stomach, looking both concerned and pleased at my words.

'I didn't even think that was possible,' I added, feeling somehow pleased with myself.

Alex smiled.

'You are generally lovely and tight,' he reassured me, 'but when you get that turned on, it can be done.'

As he spoke I realised that, though it had been a first for me, it clearly wasn't for him, and I turned my head, not wanting him to see the look of jealousy I could feel on my face. He pulled me to him, and my insecurity was gone as soon as it had come, as he buried his face in my neck.

'I love you,' he said, and I felt the rush of joy that I always did when he spoke those words. I relaxed.

'I love you. I've never felt so open with anyone.' It was true, but I couldn't help bursting into giggles as I saw the pun in my words. '. . . Especially last night.'

Alex tried and failed not to laugh with me, his shoulders shaking. I flipped him over, still giggling, and straddled him, wincing at the throb low in my stomach as I opened my legs to sit astride him. His cock rose, but he shook his head, sliding out from under me. I tumbled over, and he spanked me lightly on the ass.

'It's too soon, I'll hurt you.'

I pouted.

'So we're going to the garden centre today?'

I tried to imagine Alex wandering around perusing plants and comparing gnomes, and was dangerously close to another fit of giggles, when he pulled the quilt off me.

'No, I'm taking you to lunch. Up you get, gorgeous.'

We had sex again that night. Not quite missionary position with the lights off, but not far off. No ropes or clamps or canes at least, just long, slow, utterly satisfying sex. As I lay in his arms afterwards I was serene with happiness. The weekend might not have gone quite as he had planned but it was good enough for me; his admission of feeling less in control with me had made me feel special.

Our relationship was, I mused contentedly, pretty near perfect. The sex was off the planet, and we had a genuine friendship, total opposites in some ways but on some level connecting. I couldn't imagine going back to life before

Alex, or to a purely vanilla sex life. My submission, emotionally at least, was now complete.

At least, that's what I thought, lying content and cosy in his arms. My commitment to him, and to our lifestyle, was yet to be tested.

Chapter Eighteen

'What is it?' I walked into Alex's kitchen to find him staring intently at a piece of paper. I had a free morning, with no classes until the afternoon, and Alex had dodged out of a meeting to meet me with a cryptic *I've got a surprise for you* text message. I wondered if the paper in his hand was the surprise, but guessed not by the gamut of emotions running across his face. I knew what it was before he spoke.

'My divorce. It's done.' He waved the paper at me.

I didn't know what to say. He didn't seem overly upset, but was hardly whooping with relief either. I settled for a rather lame, 'Are you OK?'

He looked puzzled.

'Of course, I was hoping it would come this week.' He smiled, 'I'm all yours now.'

I thought you already were, I thought to myself as he leaned over to kiss me, but swallowed the words back down.

'So what was the surprise?' I asked instead.

'Ah. For that, we need to go upstairs.'

This was more like it. I sashayed up the stairs with him following, pushing my dress up over my ass. I swatted his hand away, laughing. The door to the playroom was open, and I went straight in. There, hanging from the same attachments we had so recently used, was a zebra-print swing. Almost identical to the one I had seen at the club, but a little smaller. He came up behind me, stroking my hip.

'You like it?'

I walked over to it, giving it a little push. Both sides were covered in the plush zebra print and attached to the seat there was a small leather hammock. There were cuffs high up on the side.

'How do you use it?'

'Let's find out, shall we? Take off your clothes. All of them.'

I knew that tone by now.

'Yes, Sir,' I replied as obediently as I could manage, keeping my eyes down as I slowly took off my clothes.

He came over to me and lifted me effortlessly on to the swing. It was surprisingly comfortable, the seat hugging my ass, and I held on to the sides and swung my legs out either side of him, feeling like a kid at the park. He steadied the swing with his hands and then ran one across my mouth, slipping his thumb inside. I sucked on it, looking up at him from under my eyelashes, and nipped it playfully. In response, he removed his hand and pinched my cheek.

'I think I should gag you for that. You deserve to be punished, don't you?'

'Yes, Sir. You should punish me, Sir.'

I felt the leather growing hot under my thighs and buttocks. He reached down and grabbed my ankles, lifting
and parting my legs, exposing me to him. Higher he lifted
them until my ankles reached the cuffs near my hands, and
I had to lean backwards in the swing to ease the discomfort. He tutted at me.

'Come back up. I'm going to cuff your ankles to your
wrists.'

I obeyed, feeling dreadfully exposed as he cuffed my
ankles and wrists above my head, displaying my sex in full.
I was held secure by the seat of the swing, my hands and
feet above me, my legs parted in a V. There was little room
to move. I was able to lean back just a little to ease the
stretch, but still I wished I were a little more flexible. Alex
stepped back to admire the view, his eyes lingering on my
breasts and down to my pussy and ass. I felt myself grow
wet under his gaze, and looked away, some of the old shy-
ness coming back as I hung there, legs above my head,
more open and naked than I had ever been.

He went to the drawer for the gag. I craned back over
my shoulder to watch him and the movement made the
swing rock, taking me with it. I was reminded of a ride
I had been on at the fair as a child, the same lurching in
my stomach as my body was tricked into thinking it was
in free fall. Of course, I wore rather more clothes to the
fair. Alex came back not with the simple tie I had been
expecting but with a black strap with a small round object
in the middle. I knew enough by now to know what it was:
'A ball gag.'

'Indeed. Now, open your mouth. A little wider; good
girl.'

He slipped the ball into my mouth. It was big enough to stretch my cheeks, but not enough to be very uncomfortable. Still, I felt like a pig being roasted, legs tied and an apple in its mouth. It was hardly an erotic image.

Yet as Alex knelt down and put his mouth to my pussy, I changed my mind. He licked and nuzzled me with the lightest of touches, teasing me, and the swing gently rocked, brushing me against his mouth. The way I was tied meant that it was a struggle to move the swing at all by myself; no doubt that had been his intention. He kept his hands down, touching me only with his mouth until I wriggled in frustration, which only rocked me away from his expert tongue.

I whimpered around the ball. My cheeks were beginning to ache from having it in my mouth, though I forgot about it when he finally grabbed my hips and pulled me towards his mouth, sucking hard on my clit. Exposed as I was, my clitoris felt extra-sensitive, and I hoped he wasn't going to do the whole orgasm-denial thing again, especially before work. I thought for a desperate moment that that was his plan when he stood up just as my clit began to throb, but no, he fumbled with his trousers, releasing his cock and easing it into me. I was wide open for him, both from arousal and the position he had me in. I leaned my head back, savouring the feeling of him pushing into me, his thickness inside my moist heat, the way my inner walls clenched around him, drawing him in.

He began slowly, caressing my breasts with one hand, the other on his own hip, making small movements with his pelvis. As he pushed into me the swing rocked, creating its own rhythm. I could do nothing but hang there and be rocked by the movement. It was deliciously frustrating, and when he finally began to brush my clit with his thumb I climaxed almost immediately, dropping my head back, a muffled scream coming from my mouth around the ball. Alex grabbed the sides of the swing and began to pull me on and off his cock, harder and faster, so that my orgasm exploded, subsided, and then sparked off another as I felt him pumping his own juices into me, his twitching inside me setting off my own contractions.

My limbs were shaking as he finished, and he swiftly took me out of the cuffs and pulled me into his arms, rubbing at my wrists and ankles to soothe them. Only then did I realise the cuffs had bitten into me, leaving cruel red marks. I took off the ball gag, swinging my jaw to relieve the ache in it.

'Are you OK?' it was Alex's turn to ask, looking at me intently.

I slid my hands up under his shirt, over his ridged abdominals to the downy hair at his chest.

'That was amazing. Really intense. I'm not so sure about the ball gag, though,' I confessed.

'We'll throw that one in the bin, then.'

He stroked my face, and then kissed the tip of my nose. I pushed him away, laughing, tried to jump down from the swing and went tumbling into his arms again. He shook his head.

'You have the grace of an elephant. Would you like me to help you into your clothes?'

I ignored his teasing, checking the clock on the wall.

'I need to go; I'll be late. Are you picking me up later?'

'Of course, I thought we could go for a meal? Let me make you a hot drink and a sandwich before you go.'

I rolled my eyes, although by now I had to admit to myself that I loved how attentive Alex was to my needs, and I didn't think it was just his dom training.

Before I left for work, he kissed me deeply. I sensed something, a difference in him, and frowned. Was it the divorce? His next words confirmed it, but in a way I hadn't expected.

'This is probably the wrong time to bring this up, but you do know that now I'm officially free it means we can take things to the next level? When we're ready to, of course; I'm not suggesting we go off and get married tomorrow.'

I must have looked shocked, because his next words were softer: 'I'm trying to say I want a future with you. Marriage and kids one day. The whole shebang.'

I went into his arms again, happy, searching for something profound to say.

'That's what I want, too,' was all I could manage, yet I nibbled at his neck, white picket fences and Mediterranean tanned children dancing before my eyes.

I should have known, of course. Things were going far too smoothly. The afternoon went well; I was energised from our 'quickie' – Alex's idea of a quickie of course being unlike most – and bubbling with happiness every time I thought of his words. 'The whole shebang.'

I had waved off my final class and was arranging papers on my desk when I heard the clatter of heels behind me. I sighed, expecting Amanda, no doubt trying to rope me into some more jolly after-class activities, and straightened, with a large false smile ready. Which quickly died on my face.

I knew who she was before she even spoke, the knowledge coming unbidden and unwanted into my mind. Frances. She didn't look like I expected her to; I had unconsciously expected some version of Anna, tall and beautiful yet hard-faced. But the woman in front of me was petite, with long dark hair and large blue eyes. She looked, I realised with a painful shock, like me. Only she was a more polished and glamorous version of me. Older, certainly, but the maturity in her face gave her a poised beauty. I immediately felt scruffy and clumsy and wished I was anywhere else but in front of her. The fact she had just strutted in to my classroom unannounced escaped me.

'So,' her voice was smooth as honey and dripping with menace, 'you're the girl who has been fucking my husband.'

I stepped back at the malice radiating from her, but mustered enough confidence to retort: 'He is not your husband.'

'No,' she agreed, moving closer to me. 'So you think he will be yours? A silly girl like you?'

I bristled at that. I was no silly girl. Somewhat scatty, maybe, but I held down a good job and my own home and I wasn't going to be spoken to like this. I steeled myself, looking her straight in the eye.

'How did you even get in here? I want you to leave, now, or I'm calling security.'

That achieved nothing but a derisive laugh.

'Why don't you call your boss? A bit of a cliché, isn't

it, older man and younger employee? You really think he's going to stay with you?'

She stressed the 'you' as if I was beneath contempt. I could easily imagine her as a dominant; rather too good at it, perhaps.

'Our relationship is none of your business. I'm sorry if that upsets you, but it's true. I don't know what you're doing here, but I'm really not interested in your crap.'

She just laughed again, a high girlish sound that for a moment made her look almost pleasant. It didn't last long. She stepped towards me again, her voice low and controlled, each word carefully chosen to go right for my throat.

'You're his new sub, I take it?' she said, nodding when I flinched. 'Yes, I thought so. Darling, you do realise this is all about me, don't you? Because I would never submit to him, and he couldn't stand it. When he punishes you, he's really punishing me. You'll never be me, sweetheart, and no matter how hard you try to please him, it will never be enough.'

Her words hit their mark, as if all my insecurities were on my chest like a target. For a moment I was silenced, and I saw the triumph on her face.

'Get out,' I hissed, shaking.

She left with a satisfied smirk on her face, well aware that she had done the damage she intended. I stood there for five minutes or more, staring after her, my thoughts scattered in shock, then sat down at my desk and burst into tears.

I had wiped my eyes before I got into Alex's car, but my face was like thunder. I could barely look at him as I got in, afraid I would start crying again. With just a few well-chosen words, she had completely decimated me.

'What's wrong?'

I shook my head.

'Can you just take me home, please? I really need to be on my own.'

I could tell he was dying to question me, but he did as I asked, stealing anxious sideways looks at me as he drove. When I went to leave the car without speaking, he stopped me with a hand on my arm.

'Kelly. What is it? I only saw you a few hours ago – things were fine. Is it work? Have you had bad news? Talk to me.'

'Your ex-wife came to see me.'

'Frances?' He gaped at me.

'How many ex-wives do you have?'

He looked shocked, then rubbed his hand over his chin in the way he always did when thinking hard, figuring something out.

'I did wonder if I would hear from her myself, what with the decree absolute coming through. But I certainly didn't expect this. What did she say to you?'

'She was a bitch.' I wasn't ready to discuss her theory about what Alex saw in me, maybe because I had a horrible feeling she was right. 'But never mind what she said, how the hell did she know who I was and where I worked? This is your ex-wife, Alex,' – I stressed the 'ex' – 'and according to you, the two of you had been separated for a year before we even met; she's with someone else, right? So what the fuck is she doing turning up in my classroom asking me if I'm fucking her husband?'

Only then did I realise how angry and outraged I was. I had done nothing wrong to the woman, and she was talking to me like I was some marriage-wrecking hussy? Alex also looked angry, his mouth in a grim line.

'I know my mother told her I had someone else . . . She must have given her more information than I realised. I've been talking about you to Mama on the phone; I was under the impression she was pleased. But then Frances is good at wheedling information out of people. Mama probably didn't realise she was doing anything wrong.'

I was shaking again.

'Dammit, Alex, she walked right into the room and spoke to me like I was scum. I shouldn't have to put up with this.'

'No. And you won't have to; it won't happen again.'

His voice was quiet and controlled, but I could hear the rage in it. Weirdly, he reminded me of her. That veneer of calm masking the menace beneath. They were probably perfect for each other, I thought miserably, remembering her words. 'You think he'll be yours? You'll never be enough.' I felt so tired all of a sudden. I just wanted to get in and lie down. He tried to kiss me as I left, but I offered him my cheek. He looked hurt.

'I'm sorry, it's just a shock.'

He nodded. 'I'll call you later, but please, put her out of your mind. She's no threat to us.'

I wasn't so sure of that. I let myself in without looking back to wave or blow him my usual kiss, and slumped on to the couch, pulling the cat on me for comfort even as I berated myself for being pathetic. But her words haunted me; she had voiced a fear I recognised as having been lurking in the recesses of my mind since Alex had first told me the story of his marriage. I had tried to push my insecurities to one side, and she had dragged them out and lashed me with them. And I had let her know it, too. Why hadn't I thought of a better comeback?

As I expected, my phone rang half an hour later; Alex, of course. I ignored it. After the third time, Maria tried to call. I ignored her, too. Knowing that if I didn't answer to him he would turn up, I texted to say I was going to Kim's, and did just that, leaving my phone at home.

Kim took one look at my face and poured me a large vodka.

'I've got work tomorrow,' I protested, drinking it anyway.

As I related Frances's words, she was suitably outraged.

'What a cow. What a nasty, jealous bitch. Honestly, I wish I had been there, and what a load of rubbish, anyway. How arrogant and egotistical can you get, as if everything he does is all about her? Hang on,' she paused her rant, peering at me slumped miserably in her armchair, 'you're not actually taking any of her crap on board?'

'It makes a kind of twisted sense, though, doesn't it? She even looks like me: same build, same hair . . .'

'You're talking shit,' Kim said in her usual diplomatic way; this is why she's my best friend. 'It's total rubbish. So he likes short brunettes, so what? Some men like blondes with big boobs. You're reading way too much into it. She obviously knows his tastes, has figured out that as he's so happy with you, you no doubt share them, and she's jealous. Pure and simple. She probably doesn't even want him, she just can't stand the fact he left her.'

I hugged her, sniffing back tears.

'You always know what to say.'

'Just being honest. Now, can we talk about me for a bit?'

I laughed, wiping my eyes and reaching for the vodka bottle.

It was gone two before I got a taxi home, to find a message from Alex to call him when I got in. I sent a drunk *I love you* and fell into bed, resolving not to let irate exes or my own silly fears ruin what we had.

The next day, however, I was still feeling fragile. Although I persevered with the same frame of mind and was determined not to let Frances bother me, it wasn't easy to let go of my fears. My hangover was, of course, not helping. I got through the morning by putting off the all-singing, all-dancing lesson I had prepared and throwing an impromptu test instead, while I curled up behind my desk and stared at some paperwork. When the door suddenly opened I jumped, as though I expected *her* to come swaggering back in, but it was Margaret, which was almost as bad. She had a face like thunder.

'I'd like to see you in my office at lunchtime, please,' she snapped, and then was gone.

I groaned quietly to myself. What could I have possibly done wrong now? As I walked up to her office later I ran through the list of usual possibilities, but drew a blank. I had been performing brilliantly at work; even she could find no cause to complain, I was sure. But nothing could have prepared me for the conversation I was about to have.

She was sitting at her desk frowning into space when I reached her office, throwing me a look of distaste as I tentatively walked in. Whatever was bugging her, it felt more ominous than her usual griping.

'Take a seat,' she said. Her tone was sharp.

I sat opposite her desk, feeling increasingly uncomfortable as she cleared her throat, dragging out the suspense. There was something off about her. As well as her obvious displeasure, I thought she seemed embarrassed. An agonisingly long minute ticked by as she seemed to be steeling herself to say something.

'Is there something wrong?' I prompted, looking at the wall clock.

I wouldn't have any time to grab a sandwich at this rate – not that I was feeling hungry any longer. A sense of dread was curling in the pit of my stomach.

'It's been brought to my attention that you're having some kind of relationship with one of your superiors.'

I raised an eyebrow at her. I really wasn't in the mood for this. She had seen Alex pick me up from work a few times – why ask me this now?

'Is that a problem?'

I had no idea where she was going with this. It hardly seemed a matter serious enough to be summoned to her office like a naughty schoolgirl.

'Well, not as such . . .' She cleared her throat again. 'It's more the nature of the relationship that could be cause for concern.'

'Oh?'

I had a sinking feeling, suddenly realising exactly where this was going. To say I wanted the earth to swallow me up would be an understatement.

'It has been suggested that your after-work activities may be a source of some embarrassment to the college. Some of the adults you work with are of course vulnerable and we have to be mindful of the character of our tutors . . .'

She had the grace to blush as I cut in with: 'What after-work activities, exactly?' – knowing that this could only be down to Frances. No doubt she had spread her poison while she had been here yesterday, whispering her malice into Margaret's ear.

'Apparently you've been attending sex clubs, and participating in certain . . . parties.'

My mouth fell open. I wanted to curl up and wither away then and there. *Sex clubs*? But what was I supposed to say? 'Oh, it's all right, it was just a fetish club'? I wasn't even sure of the difference myself. And in any case, it was lies. How would Frances or anyone else know about my and Alex's sex life?

Unless he had told her? The thought crept unbidden into my mind, but I discarded it instantly. No, Frances was just taking what she thought she knew and twisting it to suit herself. It was a blatant mockery, considering what I knew about her.

I took a deep breath. I could feel my cheeks flushing with embarrassment, and I knew Margaret would take my blush as 'evidence' of guilt. I was cringing with shame. Frances might have pushed her malicious gossip to fallacious lengths, but I could hardly tell Margaret the truth.

As much as I'd enjoyed my explorations with Alex, I certainly didn't feel equipped to defend that extraordinary lifestyle to anyone – let alone my boss.

Suddenly, I saw our activities through someone else's eyes, and the shine of all that wild excitement abruptly lost its glow. The private intimacy we'd shared . . . wasn't it more of a dirty secret that we'd *had* to keep hidden behind closed doors? Wasn't that why my cheeks now burned with shame? I kept my eyes fixed on Margaret's desk, my mind whirling with confusion as I tried to understand my thoughts.

And all the while I felt her cold stare on me. When I stole a glimpse at her, her expression was appalled and judgmental, cruelly dismissive. I tried to get a hold of myself. My sex life was hardly a subject I ever wanted to discuss with Margaret, of all people, but I needed to speak up for myself – or I would lose my job as well as my dignity. I straightened my shoulders and matched her icy stare with my own.

'That's not true, Margaret. I don't know where you've got your information, but it's lies.' I took another deep breath and continued. 'In any case, I don't see what my personal life has to do with the college.'

I wasn't prepared for her answer, which came immediately.

'There were complaints, this morning, from a concerned relative of one of your students.'

Oh, God. This was worse than I thought. How could I hold my head up and teach a class of adults who had also heard the rumours? This would be all round the place by this afternoon. My head was spinning. How one woman had managed to wreak such havoc in my life in less than twenty-four hours was beyond me. Nevertheless, I tried to think clearly through my emotional turmoil. I didn't see that Margaret had any real grounds to take any action. I knew I couldn't be suspended from work on the grounds of some rumour, and said as much.

'No,' she said, but there was a pause in her voice and I knew she wasn't finished with me yet. She gave me a false smile that didn't reach her eyes. 'But it might be an idea if you took a few days off. Perhaps just until this blows over.'

Until you've had time to see what dirt you can dig up, I thought. I stood up, fizzing with anger now, my embarrassment momentarily forgotten. This was desperately unfair.

'Fine. You'll find my lesson plans in my tutor file. You might want to check them for any corrupting material.'

I stormed out, leaving her door open. She made no attempt to call me back, but then I hardly expected her to.

I walked home, although it took me the best part of an hour, raging with anger and humiliation and fear of what might happen next. I wondered if anything had been said to Alex. I doubted it. His position was a lot more secure and, in any case, he was working in an office, not a classroom. For all my griping about work, I loved teaching. To have my career threatened had left me reeling. My whole life, which had seemed so settled and full of hope, now seemed as precarious as a pyramid of cards. Things had gone so very, very wrong so very, very quickly. It had only been yesterday morning that Alex was talking about us having a future; now it felt like a lifetime ago.

I got in, threw my bag down and grabbed my gym clothes, intending to take out my frustration on the cross-trainer. I was dreading facing Alex. After I had ignored him most of yesterday evening, I had been intending to apologise tonight, but now I had to tell him about this. About my humiliation, my disgrace. It was all too much.

I felt overwhelmed by emotions, burning with feelings I couldn't even put a name to. As I pounded away on the treadmill, my sense of outrage grew, and not just at Margaret, or even bloody Frances, but at Alex, too. She was his ex, after all. Surely he would have had an inkling she might try to cause trouble? I remembered my feelings of foreboding about her back in the summer. Hadn't I always known she would be a threat? And he had done nothing to protect us from her poison.

As I towel-dried my hair after my shower – my workout having brought me no peace of mind – I felt almost resentful towards him. If he hadn't dragged me into all of this in the first place, then she wouldn't have had any ammunition. If he hadn't introduced me to his unconventional lifestyle, then there would have been nothing to fear, no raging fire to set off gossipy smoke. I tried to push the thought away, but it gnawed at me all the way back home, and as I sat waiting for Alex to come round. I had texted him, telling him only that he needed to come round after work; that we needed to talk.

For the first time since we had met, I wasn't excited about his impending visit.

He paced up and down my living room like a caged lion,

the wrath coming off him like steam. When he finally stopped and turned to me, however, he looked contrite.

'I am so sorry, sweetheart. I had no idea she would behave like this, especially after so long. But it's a storm in a teacup. It will blow over.'

I gaped at him.

'Blow over? I as good as got told not to show my face at work. I've been publicly humiliated; this will be all round the staffroom. And I teach grown adults, for God's sake. Do you honestly think if they all believe I'm some sex-crazed nymph who regularly gets whipped at orgies that they will have any respect for me or listen to a word I have to say?'

He reached for me, looking concerned as he saw the tears springing to my eyes, but I turned away from him. Blow over? For him, maybe. I stood to lose at worst my career and at least my reputation. And for what? All because I had started a relationship with Alex? I was bubbling over now with the resentment I had tried to push away earlier, and I directed it straight at him.

'This is because of your shit, Alex. Your crazy ex, your kinky sex preferences. I didn't ask for any of this, and I don't want it.' I spat the words at him.

Alex sighed and looked hurt. I knew I was being unfair, but at the same time knew that what I was saying was true. The fact that I was more than a willing partner in his 'kinky sex preferences', and that this must have been as much of a shock to him as myself, didn't alter the obvious: if I hadn't been with him, none of this would have happened. I loved Alex, yes, but enough to have my life ruined? All of a sudden the job I spent so much time moaning about had become the centre of my universe. And there was something else: shame. When Margaret had questioned me about the 'nature' of our relationship, I had felt ashamed, even dirty. It was one thing surrendering to my passion for him in private and having girlie conversations with Kim and Anna, but to be publicly cross-examined? I felt sickened, suddenly seeing the events of the last ten months in a wholly different and unflattering light. What had seemed so intimate and daring in private looked sordid now it was under scrutiny.

Alex went to speak, to reassure me, perhaps, but I raised a hand to cut him off. I had gone cold, and felt myself withdrawing from him, shutting down in self-preservation. If I let him touch me I knew I would fall into his arms and sob, and that wasn't what I needed right now. I needed to be alone for a while, to try to make some sense of my feelings.

'I want you to go.'

'Kelly, I know you're upset, but I can sort this out at work, and Frances has done her worst . . .'

'Has she? So that's it now, is it, she has her little bitch and tries to ruin my life, and we just forget all about it and live happily ever after?'

'You're letting her cause friction. This is exactly what she would have wanted.'

'Do you still love her?'

The words were out of my mouth before I could stop them, before I was even aware I was going to utter them. Alex looked shocked, then baffled.

'She implied,' my mouth went dry as I repeated her words, 'that you still wanted her. That when you "punish" me, you're wishing it was her.'

'And you believed any of this?'

He looked furious, though whether at her or me I wasn't sure.

'It makes sense.' I was calm now, folding my arms, the sense of wanting to withdraw from him returning. 'After all, that was the problem, wasn't it? That you both wanted to be top? And you're still playing your silly little control games with each other. I don't want to be in the middle of this, Alex.'

He spoke to me slowly, as if to an angry child, which just annoyed me even more.

'You're being ridiculous; you know how I feel about you. I understand today must have been horrible for you, but I will get it sorted. Margaret had no right to treat you like that on the basis of a rumour, but honestly? I didn't think you would react like this over what amounts to gossip and lies.'

'It isn't just that, is it?'

'You believe what she said.' He made it a statement, not a question.

I shrugged, feeling weary.

'I don't know what I believe. Please, Alex, just leave me alone.'

'Babe, I had no idea she would do anything like this, I haven't even spoken to the woman in months. I know you're hurt and angry, but this is not my fault.'

Wasn't it? I would regret my next words for a long time, but at that moment I felt spiteful, and wanted to make him feel as small as I had earlier that day.

'You dragged me into this. You introduced me to all this. And now I have to be humiliated at work because of your dirty little fetishes.'

For just a moment he looked anguished, the hurt and shock obvious in his eyes, and a part of me longed to tell him I didn't mean it, to go into his arms and just let him take care of it, let him make things all right. But even after months of submitting my body and surrendering my heart to him, I couldn't do it.

'Are you sure this is what you want?'

I knew what he was doing; giving me an opening, so I could say 'Call me later' or 'Just give me some time on my own', but I didn't take it. I thought of Frances standing in my classroom, of Margaret calling me to her office, then of yesterday morning, cuffed to his swing, and for the first time felt no thrill. None that was worth this, at least.

'Yes. Please, will you just go?'

'Of course.'

I saw anger, then something else, something raw and painful, pass over his handsome face like a shadow. He walked out, shutting the door quietly behind him, no slamming. I didn't watch him leave. I sank down, head in my hands, but I didn't cry. I couldn't cry. I felt empty, bereft. For a brief moment I thought about running after him, telling him I didn't mean it, but what did I have to apologise for? In any case I couldn't have found the energy to move if I had wanted to; my legs felt like so much dead weight, my heart was an iron fist in my chest. Alex was gone, and even though it was against every instinct I possessed, I had let him go.

Chapter Nineteen

The next few days were torture. I missed Alex so much I could barely breathe. I picked up my journal to try to make some sense of my feelings, and just sat there staring at the blank page. Alex left it a day and then tried to call, but I ignored him. I phoned in sick at work, claiming a 'stress-related virus'. I could have sworn the girl who took the call had a knowing, mocking tone in her voice, but maybe I was being paranoid.

I wandered around my flat, restless, crying sporadically. As much as I longed to see him, I also didn't want to. It felt as though our relationship had been dirtied somehow; I couldn't think of him without hearing Margaret's disapproving voice or seeing Frances's mocking smile. I felt raw, my heart an open wound that just wouldn't let up weeping. I had never felt so wretched, and the depth of my feelings shocked me.

He was just a guy. I had been through break-ups before; I would get over this one.

But my words of self-encouragement sounded hollow even to me.

*

I don't know what to do with myself. Alex has tried to ring again this morning but I just can't face talking to him, even though I miss him so much. I'm just gutted. The things I said to him were horrible, and he's not responsible for other people's actions, is he? So we should be sticking together through this, really, but somehow I just can't. I'm terrified I'm going to lose my job, while I bet he's all right up in his manager's office, and I don't want to face anyone at work anyway. The gossip around the staffroom will be awful. I'll never live it down.

What if Frances was right? It makes a sick kind of sense. I don't want to believe it; things have been so good between us, I know he loves me, I don't believe for one minute he still has those feelings for her. But sexually? He's always said how much I affected him at first, how he could hardly control himself, and there was me thinking I was just irresistible to him, when it could have been just some hang-up over her. I know he still feels like he failed because his marriage didn't work out. Would he be back with her if she hadn't met someone else? I'm just tormenting myself.

Haven't been able to stop thinking about Alex all day today. This hurts; like, actually hurts. My tummy's in knots, my head's banging. Maybe I should just call him.

I've had enough of feeling like this. I'm going back into work, and I'm going to front it out. I'm not the first woman to get involved with her boss and I can say the rest is just rumours. Alex has stopped trying to call. Well, if he was that bothered, he could have come round, couldn't he? So forget him. I'm moving on with my life.

I miss Alex.

I went back into work after my bout of a rather vague sickness, to a sense of anticlimax. I don't know quite what I was expecting, tar and feathers perhaps, but everything pretty much ticked along as normal. The student whose mother had apparently complained, no doubt tipped off by Frances, had been moved to a different class, and none of my other learners seemed aware anything had been remiss; I even had a small bunch of flowers from one class and a 'get well soon' card, a small gesture that brought tears to my eyes. At least someone had missed me, I thought with more than a little petulance, but nevertheless as I put my flowers into water I felt happier than I had in the two weeks since Alex and I had split. This was where I belonged, not tied to crosses and hanging around fetish clubs. I pushed the sensual images that sprang into my mind to one side.

The staffroom was hardly the den of malicious gossip I had expected either. Mari, our Polish multi-lingual assistant, asked me if it was true I had been dating the HR manager. When I nodded, bracing myself for a barrage of questions, she simply grinned and patted me on the back.

'Lucky you,' she winked at me.

I couldn't help grinning back at her, though I felt a pang as I realised I could now only say I 'had been' dating the HR manager. There was little chance of me bumping into Alex at work: the HR office was the other side of the city centre and, as Alex had pointed out at our first meeting months earlier, he had next to nothing to do with my department on a day-to-day basis. Nevertheless I kept my eyes peeled for a sight of him, bitterly disappointed at his lack of efforts to contact me. I couldn't help feeling he should have done more. Was that all I was worth: a few unanswered phone calls, and then he lost interest? The fact that I wasn't sure I even wanted to speak to him hardly seemed to have any bearing on the matter. I was certainly too stubborn to contact him first. I couldn't help but compare his sudden silence to the way he had pursued me so resolutely in the beginning. If he wanted me, he would surely make it clear.

But the week went by and there was still no word from him. Being back at work made the days go by quicker, and I buried myself in paperwork and the gym in the evenings, but there was no getting away from the night-times. If I slept at all it was fitfully, tormented by dreams of him. The erotic dreams were the worst, waking up aroused but aching with loss and then turning over to an empty pillow. I missed everything, not just the intimacy, but I couldn't deny that the longing for his touch was almost acute.

I had agreed to go to a Halloween party at the end of the week with Kim, more to stop her worrying about me than anything else, and I was clearing my desk at the end of the day, wondering dispassionately what to wear, when Margaret's secretary popped her head in to inform me my presence in Margaret's office was required.

Here we go, I thought in dread as I walked up the stairs, my arms full of folders. No matter Alex's reassurances, I knew that in truth it would be very easy for Margaret to let me go; all the tutors were on short contracts that were renewed every term, and it would be an easy matter to inform me they just didn't need me after the end of this one. In practice, we were chronically understaffed and there was more chance of tutors leaving under their own steam, thanks to the hours of unpaid work that went along with the job, so I had always felt relatively secure, but this might just do it for me. I entered Margaret's office with my folders up in front of me like a shield, eyeing her warily when she motioned me to sit down. She cleared her throat, not looking at me.

'I hope you're feeling better?' she said politely.

I nodded, dumb. She knew very well I had been feeling fine until she had called me in last time. She went on in the same polite tone, still not meeting my eyes, and as I realised what she was saying my mouth dropped open in surprise.

'We are of course very sorry if you have been caused any distress. There seems to have been something of an over-reaction to some unfounded rumours. We're delighted to have you back at work and I, ah, apologise if I perhaps did not handle the matter appropriately. I was of course concerned for both your welfare and that of the students.'

'I'm sure,' I said, trying to be gracious but completely failing to hide the smirk I could feel growing across my face.

Margaret looked so contrite that I knew she must have been ordered to apologise. This had to be down to Alex. I was still smirking as I offloaded my folders in my tray and headed off to reception to sign out.

On the way home, I texted Alex *Thank you, I've just*

spoken to Margaret, adding a kiss after five minutes of deliberation. I must have checked my phone every five minutes on the way home, but there was nothing back. Had he changed his number? I was certain he would reply, even if only out of politeness. By the time Kim turned up, I was pacing the floor debating whether to phone him. She glared at me.

'You're not even ready,' she said, exasperated. I shrugged in apology as I headed off for the shower.

'You can leave your phone at home. I'm not putting up with this all night,' she shouted after me.

I stood under the water, feeling it cascade over my body, running in rivulets between my breasts and across my tummy, and wished it were Alex's hands. An unexpected sob caught in my throat. I switched the shower off and stepped out. After my exhilaration at work, I now began to think that this really was it. He had done as he had promised and sorted things out for me, but made no attempt after the first week to contact me. It seemed as though, as far as he was concerned, that was the matter done. Was it over, had I lost him for good? The thought was unbearable. I was crying as I tried to apply my make-up and had to keep starting over, wiping away the black streams of mascara that left trails across my cheeks. I could hear Kim sighing impatiently in the other room. I pulled myself together, fighting against the sudden flood of emotion that threatened to overwhelm me.

'Ready,' I called, stepping out of the bathroom and giving her a twirl.

I was preened and pampered and smiling, but Kim wasn't fooled, and neither was I. She shot me a sympathetic look that would have seemed more sympathetic had she not hurriedly rushed me into my coat and outside to a taxi.

Once in the bar, I felt horribly exposed, as if everyone could see my recent humiliation and heartbreak just by looking at me. The admiring glances I drew from two men at the bar as I angled myself into the queue I met with hard-eyed stares until they looked away. Kim tutted at me.

'What's wrong with you? You're single now, you know.'

Single. The word, one that usually came with connotations of being young and free, sounded like a prison sentence. I didn't want to be single; I wanted to be with Alex. Once again I checked my phone, which I had managed to get past Kim, and once again there was nothing.

Two Tia Marias later and we were dancing with the very same guys I had given the death-eye to at the bar. I tried to flirt, but my heart wasn't really in it. Kim handed me an elaborate-looking cocktail and winked at me, then at the guy. His name was Steve, or something similar, and he looked like a young George Clooney.

'Not my type,' I mumbled to Kim, who snorted with derision.

'Why, because he isn't ten years older than you and doesn't come with his own dungeon?'

I glared at her.

'It's not a dungeon.'

We both burst out laughing at the ridiculous retort, and Steve and his friend eyed us warily, hoping the joke, whatever it was, wasn't on them. Kim dragged me away. The rest of the night passed in a haze of dancing, drinking, giggling and flirting, and finally passing out drunk and happy on Kim's bed. I woke with the usual painful realisation that Alex was still gone, made all the worse by the accompanying hangover.

The next day I was once again in Anna's kitchen, back where it had all started, and trying not to laugh as her current client scrubbed her kitchen floor. Naked. A pot-bellied man with a weak chin and a lazy eye, I was shocked when Anna revealed him to be a local councillor, one with a hard-hearted public image that most likely wouldn't see him through the next local elections. Clearly he needed a break from his ruthless workday persona. Anna was in full dom mode, but looked tired under her make-up.

'So there's still no word from him?'

I shook my head miserably. I had given up expecting a reply to my text. It had been a feeble attempt at contact, really, but his lack of response meant I was reluctant to risk phoning or going round – something I had been tempted to do in the taxi on the way home with Kim, who had thankfully convinced me that banging down his door drunk and dishevelled at four o'clock in the morning wasn't such a good idea.

'Have you considered going to see him?' She echoed my thoughts.

I ran my hands through my hair and went over our last conversation, including my jibe at his 'dirty little fetishes'. Anna winced.

'Ouch. That must have hurt, after you had shared so much together.'

'Make me feel worse, why don't you? And then I ignored his calls . . . now I'm bitching because I haven't heard from him' – I shook my head at my own stupidity – 'and I think

I've left it too late. I just felt so humiliated when it all happened, and he was acting like it was nothing.'

But then what had I expected? For Alex to fume and cry too? He was a doer, a fixer, like most alpha males. His reaction would naturally have been to want to sort the situation, while I had slunk off with my tail between my legs.

'Have you asked yourself why you reacted the way you did?'

Anna was looking at me intently. I shrugged.

'The things she said, I guess. She made me feel I was just some dirty little bit on the side, as if what he had been doing was wrong.'

'And you think it was?'

I frowned at her, unsure what she was getting at. Anna spread her hands palm-up on the table.

'Look,' she began, 'I think this has as much to do with your own feelings about your sexuality as it has worrying about Alex's feelings for you. You think you're fine with it, but on some level you're still worried you're doing something, well, like you said to him, dirty.'

I stared at her. Could she be right?

'But I wanted it.' I blushed as I admitted this to her. 'I went along with everything, and it was amazing, all of it. It never felt wrong, or not in a bad way.'

'Still, it might be worth thinking about. He certainly might have got that impression. Have you thought about the future?'

Once again, she had lost me.

'Future relationships? Are you going to go back to what you were used to before, or would you be looking for a new dom?'

That startled me. I hadn't even considered the possibilities, being caught up in my grief for Alex. Meeting someone new wasn't something I had even thought about yet, but Anna had a point: could I go back to what I had known before? I tried to imagine a relationship with no BDSM element to it, no treading that edge between pain and desire, no sinking into that exhilarating space where all that existed was sensation and pleasure, no begging him to touch me, no submitting to his commands. Although we had mainly kept those elements in the sexual side of our relationship, rather than living the lifestyle twenty-four seven, it had been a massive element in our partnership. The thought of never having that again horrified me. Yet I couldn't imagine being submissive to anyone but Alex, either. How did you even go about finding that sort of relationship? Trawling the club or going online didn't appeal. Was that what Alex would do? He had found his previous subs somewhere, after all. I looked at Anna as an awful thought occurred to me.

'You haven't seen him at the club, have you?'

'No, of course not. You think he would be looking to replace you already?'

I felt miserable. I really didn't know. I doubted he would look for another relationship so soon, but he had his needs, and he had been doing this a lot longer than me.

'You need to try and speak to him,' Anna said softly. She reached over the table and took my hand, stroking it with her manicured red nails. 'It would be a shame to let what you two had go. I think you need to decide what it is you really want.'

She was right. I said my goodbyes, wanting to go home

and do just that: think. Talking to Anna always seemed to leave me with too much to process. I hugged her and left, stepping over the naked councillor, who was still happily scrubbing away.

I got home and took a deep breath. The urge to talk to Alex was overwhelming, and before I had even taken my coat off my hand was on the receiver. I always make important calls on the house phone, and this was as important as it was likely to get.

His house phone rang and rang without going to the answering machine. I tried his mobile, but it was unavailable. Had he indeed changed his number? I stared at the phone for a few minutes before swallowing my pride and dialling Maria. She answered on the first ring.

'Kelly, how lovely to hear from you.'

She sounded genuinely delighted, and my eyes filled with tears at the warmth in her tone.

'I was looking for Alex. I can't seem to get hold of him.'

In the following pause, a hundred different scenarios raced through my mind. When she finally said, quietly, 'He's gone home', I was relieved. It was a short-lived comfort, however.

'I don't know when he's coming back. I spoke to him the other day, and he's talking about staying over there, taking over from Pops. What the hell happened with you two?'

Characteristically blunt. I didn't know how much she knew, so I told her about Frances confronting me at work, leaving out the sexual details. Of course, she already knew I had seen her.

'She's burned her bridges with my parents now. Alex was fuming. Had his solicitor send her a letter telling her to contact none of us, including you. Accusing her of harassment. But you should know all this?'

'I haven't spoken to him,' I admitted. Maria tutted.

'Well, I'll tell him you called. He hasn't said much, but he was heartbroken. I'd never seen him as happy as he had been lately.'

'You've got no idea when he might be back?' Surely he would have given her some indication.

Again she was quiet.

'I really don't know. Last time I spoke to him, and it was only a few days ago, he was talking about not coming back at all.'

I thanked her and replaced the phone, feeling incapable of small talk. This, I hadn't expected, but why not? It was obvious he would return to Cyprus one day, if only to sort out the family business. I realised I had been expecting that, when that happened, I'd be with him. On his arm. The 'whole shebang'. It had only been a few weeks since he had said those words and it seemed an age away.

I went to bed feeling too dazed and drained even to cry; the knowledge that he was further away than I had realised – and possibly gone for ever – leaving me numb with despair. How would I ever get him back now?

Chapter Twenty

The whole of the following week, the numb feeling persisted. It was like walking around in a fog; everything seemed dulled, without colour or flavour. I was going through the motions of my day-to-day life with a sort of weary resignation. I heard nothing from either Alex or Maria, and stopped expecting a call.

Life went on. I still had to go to work, feed the cat and go to the gym, but all day I was just waiting to be able to crawl into bed and nurse my wounds. The fatigue, paradoxically, was exhausting.

The worst of it was that, after the conversation with Anna, I had realised a few things. Firstly, that Frances's words had played into my own insecurities. It wasn't Alex's fault I didn't feel I measured up – it wasn't even Frances's. My lack of confidence had just given her a bullseye shot when she chose to shoot me down.

Yet she had also brought up an ambivalence to my own desires that I hadn't even known I had felt. I had thought I'd wholly surrendered to Alex, but now I understood that some part of me had still seen it as something I did *for him*, albeit with a great deal of enjoyment. I had never wanted to admit that my need for his sexual domination was something already present, if previously unrecognised, in me. It was something I needed, too. And in keeping that distance from my own pleasure, it had been all too easy for me to blame him as soon as the shit had hit the fan. To make him feel my own shame.

Too late, I had realised that there was nothing to be ashamed of. That this is who I was, and that I loved him. Yet I had turned and run rather than defend that. I felt terrible, in so many ways. No wonder I was just going through the motions.

As my last class of the day trooped out, a few of my students looking at me with concern, Amanda came in and set a cup of tea on my desk. I mustered a weak smile.

'What is it this time? More photos? Or handing out tea and biscuits at the next meeting?' Amanda's face fell and I immediately felt like even more of a bitch. 'Sorry. Bad day,' I mumbled, reaching for the tea.

The cup was so hot it nearly scalded my hands and I jumped, knocking some over on the desk. Amanda seemed not to notice as I reached for a tissue and quickly wiped it up, throwing it into the wastepaper bin and turning back to her, trying to look alert.

'Some of us are getting together to have a bit of a send-off for Kirsty before she goes off on maternity leave. I thought you might want to come along, cheer you up a bit. You haven't been your usual sunny self.'

I wasn't aware I had ever been particularly 'sunny' in front of Amanda, whom I usually only saw at appraisals and when she was roping me into doing something. Neither did I have a clue who Kirsty was, but still, I appreciated the offer. I gave her a warm smile.

'I'd love to.'

She seemed placated, and bustled off. I sat for a few minutes, rubbing my temples and wondering if I could be bothered to hit the gym again after work. It beat spending another evening on my own with the cat. When I heard footsteps, I froze.

'Kelly?'

His voice was unmistakable. I looked up, speechless. There was Alex, both familiar and different after a month apart. He looked tanned and healthy, but with the same tiredness to his eyes that I had myself been seeing in the mirror every morning. I wanted to rush straight into his arms, but could only sit there, shocked, drinking in the sight of him.

'Er, hi. I thought you were in Cyprus?'

'I'm back,' he said, stating the unnecessary.

I nodded. I couldn't think of anything to say, and then we both began to talk at the same time. I put a hand up, laughing.

'Sorry. You first.'

'OK.' He took a deep breath. 'I've missed you. It's been unbearable. When you didn't answer my calls I thought you were still angry, and rightfully so. I waited for you to get in touch, and when you didn't decided I had to respect your wishes. Then Maria told me you had called. She said you seemed upset.'

And I thought I had hid it well.

'I was. She said you might not come back.'

'I was considering it. Then when I thought there might be a chance . . .' He shrugged. 'I thought I should come and see you. I would have waited until you finished work, but I didn't want to risk not catching you in.'

'It's OK.'

I couldn't seem to think of anything intelligent to say. He came closer, perching on my desk, and leaned over to me, moving a lock of hair from my cheek.

'You look gorgeous. I haven't stopped thinking about you. It's been torture.'

'Me too,' I admitted, glad to be finally able to say it. 'I've hardly slept. I really thought I'd lost you. I'm sorry I was so stubborn, but I was so upset, and worried about work . . .' I trailed off as he shook his head, looking contrite.

'Don't apologise, it's understandable. You were right: I dragged you into all this. Which is what I wanted to say. I love you, Kelly, and if it's too much for you, I'm happy to give it all up. I don't need the whips and the ropes and the games. Not if it means losing you.'

I was stunned. This was a scenario that hadn't even occurred to me. Was it what I wanted? The fact that he was offering me this would have seemed unthinkable a few months ago.

'You must have missed me,' I said, my feeble attempt at a joke.

He didn't smile, but leaned down and kissed me with a hunger I had desperately missed. His hands clenching in my hair brought a flood of memories and I kissed him back, biting on his lower lip. He came round the desk and pulled me up, lifting me on to it, and I wrapped my legs around him, pulling him in. He was hard, I could feel it. I grabbed his ass, pulling him against me as if I could pull his whole body into me. I never wanted to let him go again.

'Is there anyone around?' He looked over my shoulder towards the door.

I followed his eyes, thinking fast. Mine was the only class on this corridor at this time, and I wasn't expecting anyone.

'There shouldn't be.'

He grinned, kissing me again, and my hand went straight to his zip. After weeks of desperately missing his touch I was in no mood for romance, and we could talk later. I was aching to feel him inside me again.

He parted my thighs with his hands, going straight for the sweet spot, stroking me through the thin cotton of my knickers. I responded immediately, feeling myself get wet under his touch, an insistent throb of desire uncurling in my belly, my insides tightening in anticipation. I opened my legs wider, finally completed my fumbling with his trousers and released his cock into my hand. Ignoring his protests, I slid off the desk and on to my knees.

'I want to taste you.'

I slid my mouth around his cock, enjoying the feel of him against my lips and nudging at my throat. I slipped a hand into his zipper to stroke his balls, which had gone high and tight against his body. I stood up, his cock still in my hand, feeling triumphant when I saw the flush of lust on his cheeks and his eyes narrowed and dark. He was back.

I only had a moment to revel in the heady realisation that he really was back, asking to be mine again, before he turned me and bent me over without ceremony, pushing my skirt up around my waist. I looked at the door. He had left it ajar, and I had a moment's hesitation at the thought of being discovered – I really didn't need any more scandal – before the feel of him pushing into me left me not caring about anything else. He put his hand over my mouth to stifle my screams and I sucked on his fingers, remembering how much he had always loved that. But, true to his word, there was no spanking, no naughty names, just the feel and rhythm of him inside me. It was good, our movements hot and urgent, and when he reached around and began to stroke my clit I was climaxing within minutes, pushing my own hand into my mouth now to stifle my moans. He collapsed on to my back as his own orgasm rode him, groaning into my hair. As we stood and straightened ourselves I looked at him, feeling shy.

'You would really be happy with just vanilla sex?' I questioned.

He nodded, an arm round my shoulders pulling me to him. For a second it looked as though there were tears in his eyes.

'I've had a lot of time to think, Kelly, and I honestly don't care about any of that. I can't pretend I wouldn't ever miss it, but it's a small sacrifice to make if it means getting us back on track. I don't want to lose you again.'

I buried my face in his chest to keep him from seeing my own eyes watering, and he gripped me as if scared I would disappear if he let go. We walked to his car hand in hand, the receptionist looking at us with her mouth open. I grinned at her proudly.

'It will be all around the college again tomorrow,' he

warned me. I shrugged. 'But then, of course, we have no secrets to hide now.'

'It's no one else's business,' I said quietly. I was thinking hard. Alex dropped me off at my flat, promising to return with food – some things hadn't changed – after we had both had a chance to shower and change. I ran up the stairs to my door, shutting out the cold December evening, still lost in thought.

'Come in,' I called when I heard his knock at the door.

I had lit candles, dimmed the lights and poured two glasses of wine, even cleaned from top to bottom and thrown the cat out, but I knew the look of surprise on his face when he walked in had little to do with any of that.

'You're wearing your collar.'

He sounded incredulous, but a look of happiness crept on to his face, changing to surprise when I dropped to my knees in front of him. I was wearing his favourite underwear, heels, and my collar. The look of sheer lust on his face as I sank down to the carpet was unmistakable, although he tried to hide it.

'You don't have to do this,' he said, walking over to me, hand reached out as if to help me up.

'I want to. I love that you were prepared to give all this up, for me, but there's no need. It's not just you who needs this, Alex, it's me as well. I'm sorry for the way I acted. It was a shock.'

'It's fine. I should have been more understanding.'

'No, Alex; *I* should have been more understanding. Of myself as much as anything else. I thought I had given myself to you, had surrendered to you, but I was just playing games. Playing a part. I can see now. I was always holding back, doubting myself and you.' I wasn't just talking about the sex and he knew it. 'I'm ready now. I'm all yours.'

His hands twitched at his sides, as if he didn't know what to do with me. I had never known him be so hesitant. I looked up at him, my hands on my thighs, opening my knees.

'I want all of you, Alex, with or without all this. But I miss the way we were.' I bit my lip. 'I miss the way you used to punish me . . . Sir.'

It was enough. He closed the distance left between us and pulled my head back by my hair, pulling at the side of my lips with his thumb.

'And I will punish you. Hard.'

He had me up and over his knee as he sat back on the couch in one swift motion, bringing his hand down hard on my buttocks. I yelped in both pain and delight; it had been far too long. He brought his hand down again, and again, and I wriggled helplessly on his lap, my breath coming in short pants.

'Don't you ever leave me again, do you hear me?' He spanked me again, hard.

'No, Sir,' I said obediently, and smiled to myself.

I wasn't going anywhere this time.

Let the games begin . . .

Acknowledgements

To my brilliant agent, Isabel Atherton of Creative Authors, for taking a chance on me and answering my endless questions.

To Kate Moore for her insightful editing.

To Jayne, Ann, Lisa, Annette, Julie, Dave, Hannah and all the other members in the Derbyshire SGI who have supported me. Thank you for all the positive energy! *Nam-myoho-renge-kyo*!

To everyone mentioned in the narrative – you gave me a story to tell.

To Mrs Lapworth – for encouraging the shy little girl at the back of the class to follow her dreams. Mrs Hawthorne – for doing the same for the rebellious teenager at the back of hers!

To Callum and Alannta – just because I love you.

Last on the list but first in my heart – Darren Rollins. Who now knows more about books than you ever wanted or needed!

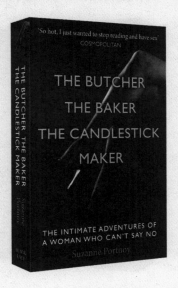

Also available from Black Lace:

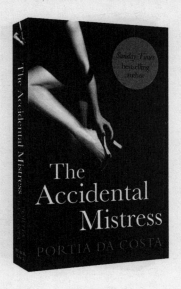

Seduced by a billionaire...

After being mistaken for a high-class call girl when they first met, Lizzie now enjoys a fiery relationship with John, her gorgeous and incredibly rich older man. Devoted, romantic and devilishly kinky, John knows exactly how to satisfy her every need.

But John has a dark side – and a past he won't talk about. He might welcome Lizzie in his bed – and out of it – but will she ever be anything more than a rich man's mistress?

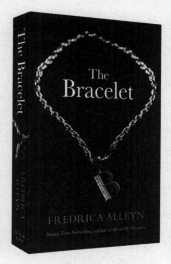
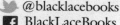